THE SCARECROW & Lady Kingston

ROUGH JUSTICE

ROUGH JUSTICE

ROUGH JUSTICE

I0659628

...a paranormal detective story

TRISTAN VICK

REGOLITH
PUBLICATIONS

REGOLITH
PUBLICATIONS

A REGOLITH PUBLICATIONS BOOK

THE SCARECROW & LADYKINGSTON: ROUGH JUSTICE
Copyright©2015-2016byTristanVick
Third edition, October 3, 2016.
All Rights Reserved.

Edited by **Monique Happy Editorial Services**

Cover art by: Tristan Vick.
Please visit Regolith Publishing at:
www.regolithcomics.com

ISBN-13: ISBN: 978-1-950106-13-4
ISBN-10: 1-950106-13-4

All rights reserved. This eBook is licensed for the personal enjoyment of the original purchaser only. This eBook may not be resold or distributed to other individuals without the prior permission of the publisher or author. Thank you for respecting the hard work of this author. This book is a work of fiction. All characters and events portrayed in the novel are fictitious products of the author's imagination. Any resemblance to any actual person, living or dead, is purely coincidental.

For my father, Wayne L. Vick,
who always believed in me and who bought me
my first laptop computer.

Contents

CASEFILE:1

Café Crunch and the Hollywood Express

CLASSIFIED

1

Cogitating Over Coffee

BUZZING WITH AN ELECTRICAL HUM, THE ART-DECO-STYLE "Danny's Donuts" sign glowed in bright neon and rotated high above the humble diner. The '50s-style glass doors of the restaurant swung open, and a gorgeous, raven-haired woman stepped into the diner with a seductive swagger. Looking over the rims of her oversized sunglasses, she glanced at all the eyes focused on her and tossed her feathery hair back. Peering between her bangs and the rims of her shades, she spotted the woman she had come to meet, pushed her shades back, and stepped urgently toward her contact.

An athletic-looking brunette with green eyes sat at the center booth in the middle of the diner. She wore a black Emily Strange shirt with the phrase "There's no place like alone" written on it.

As Julie Kingston sipped her hot coffee, she noticed increased chatter. She looked up to see the Hollywood actress Kateland Rameses Beckensale approaching. The starlet leaned over, kissed Julie on both cheeks, and sat across from her.

Smoothly sliding her sunglasses off, Beck looked around the diner, adjusted the top of her white Gucci summer dress, and broke the ice with some meaningless chit-chat.

"God, I hate L.A. in the summer," she said with a raspy yet sultry voice—the kind of voice that only comes with genuine sex appeal and smoking a few too many cigarettes.

Picking up the menu, she promptly began fanning herself with it. Her attention drifted to Julie's cup of Joe, and she jutted her chin at it, inquiring, "What are you having?"

Looking slightly annoyed, Julie smiled with a false air of nicety and told her, "It's what I always have, Becky. Coffee, black, with two creamers and one lump of sugar."

"Yeah, I won't be having that," Beckensale said, emphasizing the last word as if to say plain old coffee wasn't sophisticated enough for her taste. Looking at Julie, she smiled and leaned back in the booth, stretching her arms across the back of her seat. Beck thrust out her substantial, yet mostly artificial, chest and eyed Julie with her trademark dark, painted eyes, her bottom lip caught between her teeth.

It was the sort of look Julie didn't care for because, for the life of her, she couldn't read it. It was overly sensual and seductive for no reason, and she couldn't guess Beck's intentions. As a detective in L.A., Julie excelled at reading people. Beckensale was different, though. For some reason, Beck was impossible in every meaning of the word. Julie couldn't seem to get a handle on her.

Take the erotic chewing of her bottom lip, for example. Julie didn't know whether she was judging her silently or coming onto her. Before Julie could break the awkward tension with some trivial formality, a blonde server strolled up to the side of the booth to take Beckinsale's order. Before the waitress could take her order, however, Beckensale stated precisely what she wanted.

"I'll have a caramel Frappuccino with non-fat whip."

Rapping her fingers on the order pad nervously, the waitress leaned in and penitently whispered, "I apologize, Ms. Beckensale, but we don't serve that kind of coffee here."

"What?!" Beck gasped in an over-dramatic display of disbelief. "It's summer, for crying out loud! Besides, who doesn't serve a Frappuccino in this day and age?"

"I'm sorry, ma'am," the server replied. "I can get you a coffee with some milk or creamer if you'd prefer."

"Fine, I'll have that," Beck said in disappointment. "But just one creamer and one lump of sugar—I don't need the extra calories." The waitress curried off, and Beckensale looked back at Julie and smiled again.

Julie was still wondering what on God's green earth Beckensale wanted. She cradled her coffee cup in both hands and stared intensely back at Beck to match her overly intense gaze.

"What?" Beckensale inquired with annoyance as she began chewing on the plastic frames of her sunglasses.

"Becky, you realize you ordered the exact same thing as me, right?"

"So?"

Julie decided to let it go.

"FYI, Kingston, I just go by Beck now. *Becky* is so high school cheer squad. Do you know what I mean?"

"No, I don't know what you mean, Beck. And, to avoid seeming overly discourteous, I haven't seen you since the last annual policeman's ball when you had your arm draped around Senator Brickman."

"Blackman," Beckensale corrected. "I was with Brickman the year before."

"Whatever. Brickman-Blackman, you could be dating Batman for all I care. What I don't get is how you can waltz right in here, sit down across from me, and act like we're best friends, as if nothing ever happened between us. So, you'll have to excuse my manners. Please, go away."

Beck's dark, smoldering eyes intensified as she raised an eyebrow. "Oh my god. Are you still bitter about that? That was back in college, for crying out loud!"

Beck shifted in her seat and fidgeted with her top, her distracting cleavage forming a sloping M-shaped arch that faded into a valley of perfectly tanned skin.

"Unlike some people," Beck groaned, "I have learned to forgive and forget."

"What do you mean, unlike some people? "Julie scoffed. "You're the one who slept with *my* fiancé!"

"Goddammit, Julie Angelica Kingston! What do you want from me?"

"An apology would be nice," Julie said through clenched teeth.

"Okay, have it your way. I'm sorry!"

"That's better," Julie said, half-shocked that she'd gotten an apology from Beck.

"I'm sorry your fiancé found me so irresistible."

Julie rolled her eyes so hard that she could practically hear them tearing out of her sockets.

"I'm sorry that it ended up in a messy threesome. And I'm sorry for not pretending that I didn't enjoy it. I'm sorry for liking sex, like, *way* too much. And I'm sorry if that fact offends you."

"First off, far too much information, Beck. Secondly, a threesome? Seriously?"

"Ju, how long have you known me now?"

"Sometimes I think perhaps *too* long."

"Long enough to know that modesty and propriety are not my strong suits."

"True."

"Believe me, I'm sorry to break it to you, but your fiancé was a cheating scumbag."

Julie couldn't think of anything to say. She still had trouble grasping all the new information she had just learned. They revealed truths about her past that weren't entirely how she remembered them.

Still, the one thing she could count on was Beck's unrelenting candor, and although it killed her inside, she knew Beck was right. All the signs had been there. She'd just refused to heed their warnings.

"In a way," Beck began as she brushed her hair from her eyes, "you owe me for finding him out and saving you the trouble."

"As hard as it is for me to admit it," Julie opined, "I think you're probably right."

"So, are we friends again?"

"I suppose," Julie answered, still half in shock.

"But that's not what I came here for," Beck said.

"Somehow, I had already guessed that."

"I've come to tell you something important, Ju. I've found new meaning in my life. A purpose, you might say." Beck gazed intently at Julie, waiting for some acknowledgment.

Glancing briefly through the window, Julie turned back toward Beck and said, "Sorry, you lost me."

She waved her hand as if brushing away Julie's dismissiveness, then leaned over the table and continued in a hushed voice as if they were discussing classified information. "The world is full of sinners."

Julie blinked a couple of times. Finding it difficult to hold her interest in continuing their conversation, she replied in an equally secretive whisper, "My coffee is getting cold."

Looking irritated, Beck sat up. Her posture became rigid. She slammed her fists down on the table, her bodacious bosom standing at attention, and snapped, "Forget the damn coffee and listen to me for a moment. I'm going to share my secret with you."

"This ought to be good," Julie responded sarcastically, looking briefly into the dark vortex of her mug and waiting for Beck to enlighten her. Julie looked back up only to meet Beck's stone-cold stare. The two women stared at each other, their gazes fixed. Growing impatient with the overly long, overly tense, and overly mean silence, Julie spoke up, "Which is...?"

"I had an epiphany, Ju. People seek leadership in these uncertain times. They yearn for a bedrock of stability they can rely upon. People need to believe in something, Ju. The world is full of doom and gloom, and in these troubled times, people seek heroes, much like that old, deceased dude that everyone worships. The one who's always carrying around those railroad ties."

"Do you mean Jesus?"

"Yeah, that's the guy."

Julie placed both hands on the temples of her head and began rubbing them with her fingertips to help alleviate the sudden headache she was feeling.

"People want hope. They're desperate for it."

Adding the second cream to her coffee, Julie watched as the subtle swirls of cream spiraled around like a miniature Milky Way galaxy in her cup. "So let me guess... you're going to be the one to lead us all to the Promised Land?"

"Something like that. I will teach them how to take their destinies into their own hands. I will teach them how to bend the universe to their will. They only need a little positive thinking in their lives."

"Right. So, you're just going to walk down from the Hollywood hills, the Academy-nominated actress, and teach everyone the new and improved Decalogue?" Julie asked with a cynical smile.

Beck stood up and placed her hands firmly on her hips. "First off, I'm a two-time nominee. Thank you very much. And secondly, I don't know what a decalogue is, whatever that may be.

"Yeah, I got that." Julie couldn't help but smile at the Gordian complexity of their whole conversation.

"Oh, you just think you're so much better than everyone else, with your one hundred eighty I.Q. and your irresistibly tight ass, but I have news for you, missy." I'm going to share my secret with the world."

"Great," Julie replied in a droll monotone.

"And you know what? They may not worship me like that zombie fella, but I can help change lives! Please don't say I won't because I will. You'll see."

"Again, his name was Jesus."

"Go*, Kingston! Why do you have to be such an owner?" Waving her hands in the air, making small circles, Beck added, "Your negativity is overwhelming." It's like a black hole that sucks all the positivity out of the air and turns everything into a void as black as your empathy-starved soul."

"Right then. Well, as generous as it is of you, Beck, and as interesting as this conversation has been, I was wondering, before your busy schedule of bringing enlightenment to the multitude, could you be a godsend and with your superior f@#king wisdom, knowledge, and almighty powers," Julie said, holding up her coffee cup toward Beck as if it were a peace offering, "warm up my coffee for me?"

Taking offense at Julie's obstinacy, Beck slammed her palms down onto the table. "Of all people, I thought you'd understand. If only you knew how much your indifference hurts me." Wiping a tear from her eye, she turned and stormed off.

Julie shrugged and looked back down at her coffee. It had turned into a creamy *café au lait.* Just then, Beck stormed back up to the side of Julie's table and wagged an angry finger in Julie's face. "Just a little FYI, this is not how friends treat each other!" And she stormed off again.

Julie closed her eyes, took a deep breath, and rocked her head from side to side, attempting to loosen the tension in her neck. Although she didn't want to admit it, she still resented Beckensale.

It wasn't just the fact that Beck chose to sleep with her ex-fiancée either, cheating scumbag or not. However, more infuriating still, for all the wealth and fame she'd amassed in becoming Hollywood's little darling, she didn't have the sense to do something genuinely forthright with her fortune and fame. Instead, she merely catered to weak-minded, new-age superstitions about bending the universe to her will through the power of positive thinking. And if there was something Julie hated more than pseudo-religious quackery masquerading as self-help, it was the dupes who fell for it.

An inquisitive voice spoke out. "Was that who I think it was?"

Julie smiled at the sound of the familiar voice, but kept her eyes closed. Letting out a heavy sigh, she answered, "Yeah." Opening her eyes, she turned and looked up at her partner, John Scarecrow.

"What's the matter?" John asked in a worried tone. "You look relieved to see me."

Julie laughed at John's joke. He always knew just what to say when she was in one of her moods. "You know, you can be a bit of a stitch-up sometimes."

"Well, I try my best, although it's not a skill that comes naturally."

Julie's eyebrow raised a notch. "Oh yeah, and what skill would that be?"

"Why, my sense of humor, of course."

"Ah, I see."

"I went a year without one."

"You did, did you?"

"Lacking a sense of humor, I had to compensate with dashing good looks." John grinned as he lifted his fedora and ran his fingers through his starchy hair.

John fancied himself a hard-boiled detective, like Black Mask or Dick Tracy, and dressed to look the part. Along with the fedora, he wore a long, charcoal-gray trench coat and black leather gloves that helped conceal his strange nature while giving him that trademark Holmesian inscrutability.

"Right," Julie laughed. "So, if you don't mind my asking, how did you develop your sense of humor?"

John pushed the brim of his hat up with his thumb and leaned forward as if he had something vitally important to share. "Well, I could tell you, but then I'd have to kill you."

"Uh-huh," Julie replied with slight disappointment. She had hoped to keep the friendly banter going.

"I'd hate to have to kill you, you know? After all, you were just beginning to grow on me."

"Don't worry, I won't pry any further. I'm fond of living. You can keep your little secret."

"Speaking of secrets, what did the famous Kateland Rameses Beckensale want? It looked important."

"Nah, not really. She found enlightenment or some shit. I don't know, I wasn't listening." Julie motioned for John to take a seat across from her.

A different server with stunning red hair and an inside-out French fishtail braid came over to top off Julie's coffee and looked at John inquisitively. He waved her off with a charming smile, then put it on the table. His mind still fixating on Beckensale, he said, "She's looking as—"

"Top-heavy, ever?" Julie interjected.

"I was going to say, Lussy."

"*Slussy?*" inquired Julie with an inquisitive look.

"Yeah, you know? Classy, but also slutty. Slussy."

"Well, that," Julie acknowledged. "Did you just make that up on the spot?"

"Yeah, well, it sounded better than clutty."

"Oh, most definitely," Julie agreed. "Clutty doesn't sound sexy at all. Sounds more like a hot mess if you ask me." Her gaze shifted back to her coffee cup, which she cradled in her hands, and again became lost in thought. Looking back, Julie asked, "Have I ever told you about the Zen of brewing coffee?"

"I didn't even know there was such a thing," answered John.

Looking up at him, she smiled. "Well, there is, my friend. And I'm looking for the one—the perfect cup. "Julie slowly raised the coffee toward her lips, closed her eyes, and took a deep breath. The scent of roasted beans filled her head, causing her to smile with the realization that the wait would soon be over.

"Do you think you'll ever find it?"

Pausing, Julie opened her fetching green eyes and looked back at her partner. "There's only one way to find out," she replied, slowly bringing her cup to her lips. Just as hot coffee dampened her soft upper lip, her cup exploded in her hands like a dropped egg.

"Mother-loving-lick-nuts!" Julie cursed as scalding coffee splashed across her chest.

Without warning, white shards of the ceramic coffee mug slid through the air like jagged leaves falling in cinematic slow motion as Julie's training kicked in. She immediately slid out of the booth and hit the ground.

A sudden stream of consecutive bursts pierced the front row of windows, fracturing the glass into a thousand lines and violently shattering all around—the crinkling sound of broken glass mingled with the terrified screams of frantic customers.

2

Café Crunch

USING HER FOREARM TO SHIELD HER EYES FROM THE spattering glass raining down on her, everything around her seemed to slow down, even as her heart raced inside her chest at a million beats per second.

Julie scanned the diner and reluctantly rose to her feet, forcing herself to stand in the wake of the exploding glass. Staying down would have been ideal, but civilians were standing frozen in panic, and she needed to do something—and fast.

Bullets whizzed by her head as she ran toward the counter. Cups and dishes exploded, and the lingering debris was thick with the haze of sheet rock and white dust. Standing opposite Julie, the waitress glanced down at the glass coffee pot she held as it shattered in her hand. The coffee spilled out in what seemed like slow motion.

With precise timing, Julie leaped up and tackled the blonde waitress who was returning with Beck's belated coffee. The two of them catapulted up and over the top of the counter, sliding safely behind it.

Sitting up, her back against the inside counter, Julie waved toward a group of patrons huddled just meters away, pinned down by the gunfire. She motioned for them to head through the kitchen and out the back. Without a second's hesitation, they quickly obeyed her silent orders—all except for the waitress, who continued to sit casually next to Julie as bullets ricocheted against the walls and pinged off the pots and pans in the kitchen.

Looking over at the waitress with a confounded look that said, "What the hell are you waiting for?" Julie couldn't help but feel slightly unsettled by the waitress's subdued demeanor. "Are you okay? Are you hurt?"

"Are we in a movie?"

"Pardon?" Julie asked, completely taken aback by the question. "No," Julie replied. "We're in the middle of a f@#kin' storm, that's where we're."

Thewaitress'seyesgrewbigwithfearastherealizationsunkinaf ewmomentstoolate. "You mean this is for real?"

"I'll tell you this much. This ain't any daydream, sweetheart."

"It's depressing," the waitress said with a long, drawn-out sigh, the kind of casual release of regret that didn't quite fit within the chaos.

Julie raised an eyebrow. "Yeah, it's a bummer, right?"

"The whole world is broken," the waitress continued. "Why does it have to be this way? Why can't we put aside our grievances and love one another?"

"Good question," Julie agreed as she checked the clip of her Sig Sauer handgun. Before the waitress could ask any other questions about the unbalances she sensed in the universe, her coworker, with fishtail braids, came back for her. Taking the blonde's hand, the girl with striking red hair said, "Come on!"

Julie quickly shoved them toward the back kitchen. "Now, go! Get out of here. Both of you!"

Throughout the entire first volley of bullet-mulching mayhem, John had remained seated in the booth, calmly looking out the window as bullets pelted into him. Shards of shattered glass tinkled all around when, suddenly, alone, a bullet swiftly flew through the temple of his forehead.

The bullet passed clean through, in one end and out the other. John's eyes grew as wide as a deer caught in the headlights of oncoming traffic, and it dawned on him that he'd just been shot. His face froze in time—the effects of the bullet not yet taking their full toll—then, after a long pause, he blinked. "I'm getting shot up something fierce!"

"No shit, Sherlock!" Julie quipped as she pulled a second semi-automatic Sig Sauer from her leather jacket. Julie leaped up, laid down a barrage of cover fire with her dual guns, and ducked behind the counter. She told her partner, "Instead of just sitting there filling up with lead, try making yourself useful. Can you make them out?"

Unfazed by the ordeal, John reached up and plucked a strand of loose straw protruding from his head wound, then flicked it away. "They look like your standard paramilitary mercenaries to me."

John pushed the table over for added cover with the diner wall looking like Swiss cheese, and leaned up again. Sitting with his back to the table, he noticed bullet spatters piercing his body as they tore through his torso with a padded-sounding whoosh.

John Scarecrow, being a bona fide scarecrow and all, didn't seem too affected by the newly inflicted wounds. Reaching into the inside breast pocket of his jacket, John pulled out a small needle kit and, with steady hands, stitched up the gash on his head. He contemplated what's just one more stitch to them, many that already held my burlap-like face together.

"How are you doing over there? "Julie shouted from behind the counter.

"It's the jacket I'm worried about," John replied, with a hint of remorse as he tucked his needle kit back into his inside pocket. John pushed a finger through one of his newly fashioned holes and wiggled it around. Frayed straw jutted out of his gunshot wounds, giving him a battered and worn appearance. "I just bought this jacket," he lamented.

Julie popped back up for another round of cover fire. "Don't pick at it," she cried, "that will only make it worse!" Julie emptied the rest of the rounds from her cartridge, then ducked back down, slipped the clip out, and slapped in a new one.

The gunfire momentarily ceased as the six black suits standing in the street beside the Mercedes took their sweet time reloading their weapons. Without the racket of fully automatic gunfire to fill the silence, an eerie calm settled onto the scene. But the prevailing tranquility was cut short by a near-splitting interruption.

Aloud, hissing pop followed by a hectic spray of sparks shot everywhere, signifying the end of the "Danny's Donuts" sign, which teetered precariously on its broken limb.

Then, as if on cue, the sign twisted and toppled down onto the diner's roof with a thunderous crash. Loud pops, like firecrackers going off, could be heard as the neon bulbs of the sign burst, and a spray of sparks and glass peppered everything within proximity, adding to the surrounding smoke and debris.

3

Machinist Mayhem

AFTER THE DUST HAD SETTLED, THE MERCENARIES held their fire, waiting for any movement. Turning toward his men, the squad leaders said, "Get me confirmation of the kill."

A second mercenary spoke up. "I don't see how anyone could have survived that." But just as quickly as he finished his sentence, his head flew back as a bullet pierced his cranium. He released an ignominious-sounding "Gnaw!" and his body fell to the ground with a thud.

Raising their guns, the mercenaries released another volley of fire, their weapons firing with a staccato, *bu**a-batta-bu**a-batta.*

The chime of spent gun shells tinkled on the pavement as bullets whisked through the air with a spiraling vengeance. The roar of guns blazing drowned out the white noise of the destruction as the second volley chewed up what remained of the diner.

Dark figures with sub-machine guns encroached upon the tattered remains of the diner with cautious steps. Motioning with the smoking muzzle of his weapon, the squad leader pointed at the dead body lying at their feet. "Let's not get cocky. We should probably avoid taking any more chances. "Then, using hand gestures, he signaled the other mercenaries to close in on Julie Kingston's location and confirm the kill."

Amidst the lingering grey haze, a shadowy figure avoided the mercenaries' detection altogether. It moved swiftly against the background of settling dust and smoke. As a light breeze passed by one of the soldiers, he paused and turned around to look in the direction of whatever had suddenly darted by, but he didn't detect anything.

Letting out a nervous sigh, the mercenary turned back and tried to put it out of his mind. Just then, from the dark and dusty backdrop, a shadowy figure of a threadbare scarecrow appeared. Gloved hands reached out of the haze and grabbed the unsuspecting merc from behind, muzzling him so his screams could not be heard. Both figures quickly disappeared.

The faint sound of a garbled mumble drew the others' attention, and their heads snapped in the direction of the noise. To their dismay, they saw only a vacant spot in the smoky miasma where their comrade had been.

"What the hell is going on here?" a fidgety mercenary demanded. "We're like sitting flies south here."

"Calm down," the squad leader barked. "The more you chatter, the more likely you are to give away your position."

"That's very true," a mysterious voice concurred. The mercenaries all turned toward the direction of the voice and raised their weapons.

Scarecrow stepped out of the haze and emerged into the open, making himself as plain as day. Unable to believe their eyes, the mercenaries blinked several times, then blinked again to ensure they weren't losing their minds.

"It's...it's... a freakin' scarecrow, man."

"No, just a regular scarecrow," John replied.

"What?"

"Never imagine yourself not to be other than what you might appear to others to be. What you were or might have been would have appeared to them otherwise," the Scarecrow informed them.

However, the statement only exacerbated the mercenaries' situation. They looked utterly confounded as they tried to guess his meaning.

Turning toward his commander, one of the less talkative grunts said, "Maybe if we could write it down on paper, we could figure out its meaning?"

"*Shaɩɩup!*" snapped his commander.

"Oh, are we doing quotes today?" Julie's voice blurted out from behind what was left of the diner wall. Julie stood up, wielding her dual Sig Sauer handguns. Giving her best Clint Eastwood impression, Julie said, "I know what you're thinking. You're wondering if I have what it takes. Well, you have to ask yourself, do I feel lucky?"

Half the remaining men aimed their weapons directly at Julie, while the other three maintained a fixed lock on the scarecrow. Julie matched their change and aimed at them in return. She stared menacingly down the barrel of her guns, asked, "Well, do you...punks?"

"You're outnumbered six to two," the squad leader informed her. "I suggest you surrender yourselves now."

"Over my dead body," Julie replied.

"That can easily be arranged."

Wagging his gloved finger at the leader, Scarecrow said, "Hey there, that's no way to talk to a lady."

Looking coldly over at John, the squad leaders said, "I don't know what sort of creature you are, but before this day is done, we'll take care of you, too."

JuliesignaledJohnwithanodofherchin.Scarecrowturnedtow ardthenearestmercenaryandslowlywalkedtowardhim.

"Hey, buddy, stay where you are."

Scarecrowignoredthemerc'swarningsandwalkedstraightupt othebarrelofhisgun. Pressing his chest against the muzzle, Scarecrow looked into the mercenary's eyes, assessing his resolve. Suddenly, a gunshot rang out, and Scarecrow looked down at his still-smoking chest hole; he then slowly looked back up at the mercenary with a menacing glare. After a brief, stone-cold stare, Scarecrow said, "Boo."

Dropping his gun, the mercenary turned tail and ran away while the squad leaders shouted after him, "Coward!"

Scarecrow turned toward the other mercenaries, his posture indicating that he was coming after them next. This time, they did not hesitate to pull their triggers, and soon a barrage of bullets peppered Scarecrow with a hungry fury.

Using what was left of the diner wall as cover, Julie dropped to the ground and rolled behind the chewed-up cinder block slab as chunks of wood and drywall exploded around her head. A white, chalky dust clung to her clothes and hair. As a steady stream of bullets drilled into the concrete cinder blocks just behind her head, Julie slammed in a couple of fresh clips, tilted her gun sideways gangster style, and reached around the corner to return fire.

Her final shot managed to hit the squad leader squarely in the shoulder. Although the bullet passed straight through, he looked mighty pissed. With a snarl, he said, "The only words I want to hear from you, lady, are 'I Surrender.' Do you get me?"

From behind the shrinking wall, Julie yelled back, "Why don't you crawl up your own ass and die, dick-weed?"

Her reply sent the squad leader into a rage, and he emptied his machine gun into the wall, dropped it to the ground when it was of no further use, and quickly pulled a Glock 19 from his waistline. With hammer pounding brass, he marched forward, determined to erase his mark. When he ran out of bullets, he released the clip and, in one fluid motion, fetched a new one from his ammunition belt and slipped it in position.

At the same time, John ignored the bullets pelting him left and right and opened the chamber of his revolver to empty the spent shells. He then placed new bullets in one at a time. The use worked, and some of the mercs began trying to saw him down with a chain of gunfire.

Snorting as if he was hacking up a hairball stuck in the back of his throat, John spat out a clot of mucus-coated shells onto the ground with a sounding splat. He affirmed his victory with a grin as the barrage of gunfire ceased, while dismayed mercenaries gazed down at the bullet shells encased in the gelatinous goo on the ground.

"You have got to be kidding me," one of the mercenaries said, a look of disgust spreading across his face.

John finished reloading his Magnum, then slowly turned and raised his gun. The mercs looked up at him in time to realize it was too late. The Magnum's blasts were deafening. The powerful force of the bullets impacting their body armor caused the remaining mercenaries to rise off the ground from the brute force of each shot. Their flailing bodies looked like dolls flung into the air, and each came tumbling down onto the rigid asphalt seconds later.

Finally, safe from any further threat of harm, Julie stepped out from behind the wall, trained her gun on the only man left standing, and fired two quick rounds into his upper thighs, dropping him in an instant.

Immobilized and writhing on the ground, the squad leader clutched his wounded arm and looked up to see John Scarecrow walking toward him. "Who... who are you, man?"

Scarecrow kicked the squad leader's gun away with his foot. The firearm skidded across the blacktop with an uneasy scraping noise until it was safely out of reach. John pulled out a pair of handcuffs and reached down to slap them on.

As he cuffed the criminal, he recited a piece from one of his favorite poems in an ominous voice, "The time has come, the Walrus said, to talk of many things."

4

Interrogation

HAVING LINED UP THE CRIMINALS FACE DOWN ON THE pavement with their hands securely tied behind their backs, Julie began reading the perps their Miranda rights, but with a slight paraphrase.

"You have the right to remain dumb. Whatever stupid thing your dumbasses say will probably be used against you in court of law. You have the right to an attorney. If you can't afford an attorney, you have the right to be appointed one who has nothing better to do than waste their time in the hopeless struggle to defend outlaws and morons.

Scarecrow looked at Julie with a curious expression and asked, "The right to remain dumb?"

"I was going for the double entendre," Julie replied, tossing a pack of plastic ties to John. He caught it and continued tying up the villains.

Julie looked down at the group's leader. After a brief pause, she asked, "Do you know what you are?"

"No, but I'm sure you're going to tell me," The leader grumbled.

"A coward."

"Why don't you untie me?" he replied, "and we'll see how much of a coward I really am."

Julie crouched down and smiled at him—a show of fearlessness- as she faced down her would-be killer. She waited a moment, then continued her remonstration. "As I recall, I wasn't the one who just got schooled by a girl."

"You got lucky," he muttered under his breath.

Shrugging her shoulders, Julie smiled again and continued, "Maybe so, but that doesn't change anything."

A sense of calm suddenly came over her, and Julie stopped smiling and pulled out her gun. Still crouching down, she looked into the villain's eyes and paused briefly.

"Back in the Wild West, a lawman would be justified in killing an outlaw simply for drawing on him. Lucky for you, this ain't the Wild West, so I'm not allowed to kill you by account of the law being what it is. But I promise you, if you ever draw a gun on me again, the moment I draw mine, I'll shoot you dead."

After her little speech, she holstered her weapon, stood back, and looked at her partner, then back down at the mercenary, who was looking up at her with a contemptuous gaze that rivalled hers. The hardened mercenary just smiled condescendingly and, as if to test her resolve, scoffed, "With all due respect, officer, why don't you stop wasting your words on me and use that pretty mouth of yours for something useful, like blowing me?"

Julie frowned.

"If I were you," Scarecrow interjected, "I'd choose my words more carefully. The last guy who used those words got his wish. She blew his balls clean off."

"Do I look scared to you?" the mercenary asked defiantly, putting on his best tough-guy façade.

Fuming, Julie reached into her jacket and pulled out a handheld taser from inside her breast pocket. Without warning, she jammed it between his legs and released vicious volts of crackling electricity into his crotch.

"ZZZG-NAHHG!" he howled in pain.

"You see, the thing about sociopaths is they don't typically show signs of fear. They don't have any sense of shame or guilt for the wrongs they've committed, and don't fear the consequences of their actions. So, I think you're scared of me? No. But I do think you're stupid."

Julie pulled the taser away, leaving the man clutching his crotch with both hands. After rolling her head on her shoulders and popping her neck, she slowly turned her head and shot a cold glance at the remaining mercenaries. Pulling the trigger, the taser lit up with an electric blue arc, crackling and sparking, as she taunted the others with further gonad torture. The remaining men exchanged nervous glances as beads of sweat dripped off their foreheads.

"I'm only going to ask this once," Julie said, letting the taser snap, crackle, and pop as she waved it around for a dramatic effect. "Whose sent you to kill me and why?"

Dusting off his hands, Scarecrow finished tying up the last mercenaries. "If I were you, I'd tell the lady everything she wants to know."

Picking up the squad leader by his collar, Julie propped him up on his knees, reached down with her free hand, and clamped down on his nut with a vice-like grip.

"*Arghhh!*" moaned the squad leader. The twinge of pain creased his already perspiring brow.

"I'm losing my patience," Julie said, and squeezed even harder, relentlessly crushing the man's scrotum like a bear trap.

"Okay! I'll talk," he said in a high-pitched squeal.

Letting go of his family jewels, Julie suddenly jammed the taser back into his crotch and shocked him again. The man fell back to the ground, hands cradling his thoroughly baked oysters. Julie looked over at Scarecrow and shrugged as if to insinuate it couldn't be helped.

At that very moment, the faint rhythm of Spanish hip-hop music blaring in the distance grew audible. Julie and Scarecrow looked in the direction of the sound just in time to see a low-rider, gaudy-gold 70s Cadillac convertible bounce around the bend of the street corner. The car hip-hopped its way to their position.

Easing up next to Julie and Scarecrow, the car came to a screeching halt, and with a cagey curiosity, four Chicano gangster wannabes looked around at the inexplicable display. Bodies littered the pavement. Red blotches of blood splatter decorated it like flecks of paint. In the background was a heap of destruction where the diner had once stood, and in front of it stood a pissed-off Chicana over the writhing body of a man clutching what was left of his frazzled junk.

But perhaps even stranger was the bona fide living, breathing scarecrow, eyeballing them suspiciously.

John Scarecrow calmly flashed his police badge and quipped, "Nothing to see here, folks." With the dilapidated diner still smoking behind him, he waved his hand, motioning for them to carry on, and added, "Move along, move along."

The music was turned up, and awkward glances were exchanged between the nervous Chicanos. Then, no longer hopping to the beat, the gold Cadillac idled on the road, and when it reached the corner, it immediately took a tire-squealing left, burning black crescents in the road as the Chicano gang members high-tailed it.

"That was awkward," Scarecrow stated in a bemused tone and a half-smile curling on the corner of his mouth.

"Sure was," Julie agreed. In the distance, the sound of sirens could be heard fast approaching.

5

Backlot Blues

PULLING UP TO THE SOUNDSTAGE ON THE STUDIO LOT, THE dark, metallic grey Camaro ZL1 with black carbon racing stripes stopped. Its V-8 rumbled like the purr of a magnificent panther. With a rumble, the engine shut off, and all became quiet.

Julie got out of the vehicle sporting a raspberry leather jacket, a charcoal grey tank top, and Oakley sunglasses. She pulled off the reflective Oakleys that adorned her face and scanned the empty movie lot for anything unusual. Scarecrow, having changed out of his tattered threads, now wore a three-piece suit of different shades of grey, complemented by a sharp black-tie contrasting with the muted tones.

Scarecrow shrugged his shoulders and turned toward his partner. "I must admit, you know how to put the pressure on in your interrogations. Curious, but I must ask, do you think using the vice grip was a little too much?"

Julie looked over at John with a demure grin. "Even though the toughest big shots will eventually crack under enough pressure. The only ones who don't are those willing to die for a cause. I simply deduced that as a hired thug, our man had no such predilections. So, it was only a matter of time before he spilled the beans. As for when I knew he'd crack, well, I think it's when I pulled out the Chinese finger-traps."

"You'd realize you could get suspended for pulling a stunt like that, right?"

"Look, it's perfectly legal to clamp Chinese finger-traps down to a table in the state of California."

"Not with the criminal attached to them. All three of them!"

"Oh, don't be a worrywart. Someone will eventually get him out of it."

"But what about the emotional damage?"

Julie raised an eyebrow. "Well, perhaps he should have chosen his words more carefully then."

Scarecrow shrugged and let it slide. The entire precinct didn't call her "Hot Tamale" for nothing. The nickname fit her to a T. Red. Hot. Explosive. But it was more than just her personality that made her edgy. Julie could walk the fine line between true justice and vigilantism without ever straying too far.

John knew that upholding the law to the best of his abilities was just part of his duty to serve and protect the public. At the same time, I realized there were occasions when one might have to go against the law to do the right thing. Sometimes, that was the only way to enact justice. After all, even an ambulance must speed to save a critical patient.

It was apparent to him that Julie viewed laws as guidelines rather than inflexible dictates. He was not looking to make a habit of bending the law like she was, but he understood why Julie never hesitated to do so.

"Let's see if I have this straight," John said, stroking his chin contemplatively. "The person who hired the hit is your old pal, Blake 'The Razor' McDoogle."

"That's what my informant on the inside said, at any rate."

"McDoogle, however, issecurelybehindbarsservingback-to-backlifesentencesandruingthedayheeverheardthenameJulieKin gston."

"No doubt about it."

"But he's still bitter about you preventing him from skinning any more girls alive and still has enough influence in the shady underworld of crime to reach the outside and try and erase you."

"Appears that way."

"Moreover, he harbors an unhealthy fixation with one of Hollywood's most famous starlets for unknown reasons. That starlet being none other than our beloved and dear friend Kateland Rameses Beckensale."

"Bingo."

"The question is, how deeply is she involved? Is she aiding him of her own volition, or is she being squeezed, made to do his bidding until she no longer serves a useful purpose?"

"After our bizarre conversation today, I suppose anything is possible. Something certainly had her on edge. But I don't think she would have sought me out after all this time unless it was vitally important."

"She might've been trying to warn you about the shootout."

Julie scratched an itch under her arm. Whatever the case, the only sure thing is that the rabbit hole goes deeper than we initially thought. We need to find Beck before she gets into deeper trouble than she already is."

"Well," John began, pulling out his smartphone and checking the email he received earlier. Her agent said she would be on the sound stage doing reshoots for her latest film.

"About that..." Julie paused, looking around at the empty lot. "You sure they gave you the right address?"

"I'm quadruple-checking it now," he replied, bringing up the location in Google Maps. "Um...yep. We're in the right location."

"Doesn't it strike you a little bit strange that nobody else is around?" Julie slid off her shades, tucked them into the inside breast pocket of her raspberry-colored leather jacket, and then stared into the distance.

"You thinking it might be a trap?" John inquired, looking around nervously.

"Oh, it's most definitely a trap," Julie confirmed. Putting her hand on her hip, she tossed her hair and then looked back at Scarecrow with her trademark game face. "You ready for this?"

"Not really," Scarecrow replied. "The first assassination attempt was more than enough for me. But I suppose the saying is true: Evil refuses to sleep until evil is done."

"Right," Julie replied, nodding along with the truth bombs Scary was dropping.

Off in the distance, the high-pitched wail of an old steam locomotive blared.

WHOO-WOOO!

Julie and John turned towards each other and spoke in unison, "Did you hear that?"

"I'll go check out the train," Julie informed. "You try to find anyone to talk to and see what the hell is happening around here."

"Will do, partner," Scarecrow chirped with a two-fingered salute. With that, he turned around and headed toward the massive soundstage behind them.

Julie waited until he was out of sight, then headed off in the other direction to discover why a train was running on an abandoned backlot. She'd have to descend into the rabbit hole to find any real answers.

6

Showdown

SINISTER SHADOWS STRETCHED ACROSS THE DARK PAVEMENT and crept down the drainpipes, walls, and windowsills as they followed Scarecrow, nipping at his heels as he walked past the rows of ominous buildings. Keenly aware of the growing dark, he could feel danger lurking in the deepening shadows of the backlot.

Scarecrow arrived at the central soundstage. It was the size of an airplane hangar. Light flooded the room as he pushed open the large doors that led into the massive soundstage. Even so, the room was too big for the light to illuminate fully.

Scarecrow couldn't shake the nerve-racking feeling that hidden forms lurked in the darkness of the soundstage's confines. John's silhouette stretched across the thick slice of light that cut across the entrance and quickly receded into the darkness, swallowed by the large room's dark mouth.

"Anybody in here?" he called out, his voice fading into the ample, hollow space. John waited a moment and then said, "Guess not."

Before he had time to close the doors, however, an unexpectedly large CRASH rang out from within the shadowy void.

"Who's there?" Scarecrow asked, startled, and reached for his revolver. Stepping further into the soundstage and peering intensely into the dark, he fumbled around, feeling for the light switch until he finally found it. Flipping it on, the studio lights came to life with an insect-like electrical hum. Buzzing around him, the lights steadily warmed to a soft glow.

As his eyes became accustomed to the light, John discovered he was standing in the middle of a replica of an old frontier saloon, the same sort he'd seen in old Westerns.

Looking around some more, he scanned the room. His eyes roamed over the bar, the card tables, the back wall, then back at the card tables. Standing in the center of the room, between the bar and the card tables, was a cowboy wearing a crimson bandana. He looked a lot like a classic stagecoach bandit; he sported a ten-gallon hat and looked all kinds of mean.

"Tis' here town ain't big enough for the both of us," the strange bandit announced in a cheap imitation drawl.

"I beg your pardon. "John said, his hand cautiously hovering above the hilt of his gun, which sat there ready.

"Nuh-uh!" warned the cowboy, shaking his head and eying John's hand sharply, "I wouldn't do that if I were you."

"Do what?" John asked innocently as his hand came to rest on the handle of his revolver.

"You best be keen to know that I am the fastest draw in the West."

"I know the fastest drawing in the West, and you ain't there."

"Youbetterclampthattheretrapshutlestyouwantabulletbetw eenthemgoofyeyesofyours."

"Goofy? Look, pal, I don't know you, and you certainly don't know me. So, I think it would be best if you just put those pea shooters down and come with me," Scarecrow replied sternly, involuntarily getting drawn into the line.

Abruptly, the cowboy drew his pistol and fired several shots.

BLAM!

BLAM!

BLAM!

As bullets whisked through the air, John made a little attempt to avoid getting shot and, instead, absorbed them–a luxury that only a scarecrow could afford. Drawing his own revolver with lightning-quick speed, the Scarecrow promptly returned fire before the bandit could fire again.

A couple of above-the-knee shots took the legs out from under the bandit and effectively rendered him immobile. As the bandit dropped to the ground with a wail and a thud, he lost hold of his gun, which fell to the floor and skidded just beyond his reach. Reaching for the gun, warning.

"Don't move another inch if you intend to keep that hand intact."

Reeling in hand, the bandit rolled onto his side and looked at Scarecrow. "I guess that makes me the third fastest draw," he moaned.

"I reckon it does," Scarecrow replied, straightening his back and holstering his weapon. Suddenly, there was a cough and the clearing of someone's throat. The scarecrow twirled around only to find himself surrounded by a dozen more masked bandits, each dressed like cartoonish railway hijackers. Raising his hands as if to surrender, Scarecrow said, "Hi there, fellas. How can I assist you?

The bandits didn't say a word. Instead, all twelve reached behind their backs and drew wickedly sharp samurai swords.

"Katanas?! You've got to be kidding me," Scarecrow said, bewildered at why railway bandits would bear armed likenesses of ninja assassins. Putting his arms down, he flipped over his badge and showed them he was an officer of the law. "Hold it right there. Police."

A moment passed as they all simultaneously glanced at the badge, then back at him. After an intense silence, the leader, still writhing on the ground in pain, motioned with his chin for his posse to advance. Like a hungry pack of piranhas, the posse moved in on their target, their razor-sharp blades extended like spears.

"Usually that seems to work," John said disappointedly as he tucked his badge back into his inside breast pocket. Suddenly, a whole series of sharp blades, all aimed at his throat, surrounded him from nearly every angle.

Grasping his leg, the bandits' leader used the bar counter to help him stand up. Looking at Scarecrow, he asked, "Any last words before you meet your maker, you beady-eyed sock puppet?"

Scarecrow slowly scanned his attackers' dark, piercing eyes and said, "Shall we stop dillydallying and get this show on the road?"

Blades slashing down upon the straw man from all directions. Taking defensive action, Scarecrow leaped onto the bar and kicked the leader in the head, which sent him crashing back down to the hardwood floor. He continued, sharp blades slashing viciously at his Achilles heels.

Scarecrow reached the end of the countertop and leaped to safety. Grabbing hold of the room's full-scale, replica crystal chandelier, he swung over the card tables, narrowly avoiding the cold bite of steel that nipped at his heels. Breaking away just in the nick of time, Scarecrow swung away to safety.

Landing on the other side of the tables, the Scarecrow turned to see a wall of menacing, masked marauders blocking him. Since going back, the way he'd come was out of the question, he looked around for an escape. But it was no use. There were no more visible exits.

"Ah-ha!" the bandit leaders said, rising up again. "You're just like General Custer, trapped between a rock and a hard place, or in this case, imminent death!"

Scarecrow's face tensed up into a frown. She didn't like the analogy much. "It seems you may be right," Scarecrow admitted. With nowhere to go, Scarecrow looked up and spied the walkway that led to the lighting fixtures. He followed the catwalk until it met the wall, where a ladder was located at the back of the soundstage. Relief swept over him, and he dashed toward the ladder and started climbing. An angry mob of bloodthirsty bandit assassins trailed after him, hot on his tail, and he made his way to the roof.

WALKING DOWN THE CENTRAL STREET OF AN OLD FRONTIER town, Julie Kingston turned the corner by the post office at the edge of the boarded-up ghost town. She ran into an Egyptian desert scene replete with fully detailed one-fourth scale model replicas of the Sphinx and the Great Pyramids. It was a bit surreal to see an American frontier village overlooking the Great Pyramids of the Egyptian empire, and she couldn't help but wonder what in the hell kind of movie Beck was making.

Julieraisedherhandandsquintedagainstthebrilliantsunlightt hatbouncedoffthewhitesanddunesofimportedTunisiansand. A flock of black crows flew overhead, cutting across the blue sky.

From behind the Sphinx, the silhouette of a busty cowgirl stepped out and casually lit a cigarette. "If you're wondering what time it is..." the figure said. "It's about half past."

Julie redirected her gaze toward the mysterious voice but couldn't glimpse the woman's face. The woman finished lighting her cigarette, took a long drag, then puffed out a haze of smoke. A long shadow cast by the Sphinx splashed across the mysterious woman's face, concealing her true identity.

"Do you reckon?" Julie asked with an air of sarcasm.

"Ah' do reckon," the shady figure replied in a sultry southern accent that seemed to come and go as it pleased.

Julie paused. Deciding it was probably best to be cautious, Julie pulled her jacket open, flashed her badge perched just above her hip, and inquired, "Is there anything I can assist you with?"

"Ah was gonna ask you the same thing, darlin'."

Kateland Rameses Beckensale emerged from the Sphinx's shadow dressed in slattern cowgirl garb. Julie gasped, "You?!"

7

The Great Escape

KATELAND RAMESES BECKENSALE STEPPED INTO THE LIGHT, silken strips of her smooth bare legs peeking through her leather chaps. She was dressed like a mix between a cowgirl and a prostitute. Along, tan, tattered duster completed her ensemble, and her coattails flapped in the breeze, revealing black bikini bottoms under her leather chaps.

"That outfit is not historically accurate," Julie observed. Beck just stared back at her with a blank look on her face. Julie continued, "I mean, the tight cut of the leather vest seems designed only to maximize your cleavage, and the way that it reveals your flesh midriff doesn't seem to fulfill any useful purpose either. In all honesty, it looks like a second-rate cosplay outfit."

Nudging the brim of her cowboy hat back, Beck coolly took the cigarette out of her mouth, blew a couple of smoke rings, and flicked it away. "Oh, by little faith, this outfit serves an instrumental purpose."

"Oh? And what on Earth could that possibly be? "Julie asked.

"To annoy you. Obviously. Besides, you're one to talk, Kingston."

"What does that mean?"

"You always dress so inappropriately."

"Inappropriately?" Julie looked down at her leather jacket and tattered blue jeans, with tears across her thighs to add a touch of sex appeal. "What are you talking about? This is an outstanding outfit for a plainclothes cop to wear.

"Yeah, a cop from Chicago, maybe. And you're wearing a leather jacket in the middle of summer. It's L.A. for God's sake!"

"Well, Miss Priss, why don't you take me shopping next time you go, and you can pick my outfit for me!"

"Fine. Will!"

"Fine!"

"It's a date then."

"Fine!"

Beck and Julie shot each other irritated looks, but both women were secretly excited to have unintentionally made an impromptu shopping date with one.

"So what are you doing here, Beck? You have some explaining to do."

Out of self-conscious habit, Beck readjusted her cowgirl's hat again. "I have something important to tell you."

"What would that be, exactly?" Julie asked impatiently.

"My epiphany, I told you about earlier. I had another one!"

"You did, did you?"

"It's time to cleanse the world of all the weak sheep, Ju. Survival of the fittest and all that. The day of reckoning is upon us."

"What in bloody hell are you on about, Beck? Yousoundlikeagoddamnedtele-evangelicalinfomercialforreligiouscrackpots."

"I'm talking about the Judgment Day, Ju. The day the sheep will be separated from the goats. The day we learn the truth about who is worthy and who isn't."

"If you mean the Rapture, then I pray you're right, and I sincerely hope you float the f@#k off. I'll even throw in a heartfelt amen after you're gone."

"Mock me if you will, but the time for you to choose is at hand!"

"A choice?"

"In my vision, the zombie guy spoke to me."

"Zombie guy? You mean Jesus?"

"Yes. Zombie Jesus spoke to me."

Julie sighed and buried her face in her palm. "I know I'm going to regret asking this, but what did Zombie Jesus say to you?"

"He said: *Let not Kingston suffer.*"

"What does that mean?"

"I don't know. It was a pretty wild vision. Also, I was well, you know…" she motioned as though she were taking a hit from a blunt and then continued, "It's still all a little hazy, if you know what I mean." Beck giggled, then added, "I think I might still be a little bit high."

"You think?" Julie equipped.

"But I know this much," Beck continued. "Zombie Jesus said he wants us to be together. He doesn't want you to suffer alone."

"That's very considerate of him," Julie remarked with her usual amount of snark.

"Join me," Beck said, extending her hand and offering it to Julie. "Join me, and I can help you end your suffering."

Julie just squinted at Beck as if she was contemplating whether she was just Hollywood crazy or bat-shit insane. Although she thought the difference probably didn't matter all that much.

"Just look at yourself for a moment. You're as high as a kite, dressed like a cowgirl prostitute, and your breasts are practically falling out of your vest. It's ridiculous."

Beck looked down and groped her breasts, squishing them together and letting them playfully bounce back.

"Are you kidding me?" Beck asked conceitedly. "I look f@#king fantastic! I've got tiger blood, babe."

Julie merely rolled her eyes. Just another typical day in L.A., Julie reminded herself. All you can do is learn to live with the crazy.

"I sense great confusion and anger in you. Anger leads to hate. Hate leads to darkness. Wash the darkness from your soul, Julie! Confess your sins to me and be absolved." Beckensale quickly drew a pistol from the holster on her thigh and steadily aimed it at Julie. With a wild look in her eye, jaw clenched, she added, "Or perish!"

"FYI, I don't like being threatened by a maniac with a gun, so why don't you do me a favor and take this middle finger I'm giving you and shove it up your…"

BANG! A bullet whisked by Julie's ear.

"For Pete's sake! That was a real bullet that just whizzed by my head!" Julie yelped.

"Wow! What a rush!" Beck laughed giddily. "I think I'm beginning to understand your preoccupation with the long arm of the law." Holding the smoking barrel up to her lips, she blew, just like in the movies.

"You crazy bitch!" Julie screamed. "You could have f@#king killed me!"

"You're not listening to me!" Becky yelled with the ferocious rage of a woman ignored, and she fired another couple of poorly aimed shots.

BANG!
BANG!

Julie ducked, tucked, and rolled. The bullets missed their mark by a wide margin. Out of imminent danger, Julie rose upon one knee and aimed her gun squarely at Beck. "Drop it!" Julie ordered authoritatively. "Or I pop those precious items of yours."

Clutching her chest as if she were protecting a precious baby, Beck stared back fearfully. "You wouldn't dare."

"Try me."

Beck assessed the situation, thinking for a moment. She looked down at her beautiful breasts, and without any further hesitation, she threw her revolver away and made a break for it.

"Oh no you don't, you crazy zealot bitch!" Julie yelled, springing up to grab the coattails of Beck's duster jacket. To her chagrin, Beck easily slipped out of it and continued her escape, making a beeline toward the pyramids.

DASHING ALONG THE ROOFTOP OF THE SOUNDSTAGE, DRY gravel crunched under Scarecrow's feet. Approaching the rooftop's edge, Scarecrow dug in his heels and skidded to a halt. Straw poked out of the jagged edges from where the blade had sliced him. Pieces of straw fell to the ground. Surprisingly, he managed to keep it together, but barely.

Off in the distance, the sound of a steam locomotive could be heard drawing nearer and nearer as the horde of angry bandits closed in on him. Scarecrows pulled out his revolver. Cautioning them, he warned, "Don't come any closer, or I'll open fire!"

Winding back his arm, the lead bandit stepped out in front of the pack and launched his katana like a javelin. Everyone paused as they watched it sail through the air. Even John stopped to watch the hurled projectile slowly arc through the sky, holding his revolver steady. Scarecrow raised his gun at the sky.

Slowly, as if caught on high-speed celluloid, the sword slid through the barrel of John's gun, splitting it in two, and then just as easily lodged itself into John's chest. Looking down at his impaled torso, John threw down his split side arm and examined the craftsmanship of the samurai sword. "Must be Japanese," he said to himself.

John spun back around and made his way over to the edge of the soundstage rooftop with the sword hilt still protruding from his sternum. Looking slightly unsettled, Scarecrow crept up to the brink and looked over. The building seemed a lot higher than he had initially imagined.

The bandit assassins pressed toward him until they had pinned Scarecrow against the rooftop's edge. Slowly, they extended their swords and aimed their blades directly at the man of straw.

The locomotive's whistle blared with a resounding "Whoo-woo!"

The sound was so loud that it seemed the train was on top of them. John looked at his assailants and gave them a laid-back two-finger salute, then, without a moment's hesitation, he jumped over the ledge.

Running up the rooftop, the bandits looked down over the ledge only to see John grinning back as the masher rode away atop one of the speeding locomotive's passenger cars.

Following after him, the first bandit overshot the train entirely and howled before disappearing out of sight. The rest of the pursuers fared better and landed securely on the moving train. Securing their footing, the bandits drew their weapons and ran along the top of the cars, making their way toward Scarecrow.

John struggled to his knees and grabbed the sword's handle that protruded from his body. Like a hardened warrior, unshaken by years of battle, he tore the sword from his chest and slowly rose to his feet.

Swinging the blade out to his side, Scarecrow cut the air with the sharp, menacing sound of steel hardened for battle. Looking at the men shambling along the top of the train, Scarecrow let out a warrior's cry. The two forces charged toward one.

JULIE CHASED BECK UP THE REPLICA PYRAMID. THE TWO looked like giants stomping over the Great Pyramids of Giza. Upon reaching the top, Beck slipped and tumbled down the backside, screaming obnoxiously the whole way down.

Julie paused at the summit and watched Beck slide to a halt, landing at the bottom of the pyramids near the edge of some railroad tracks. Suddenly, a train whistle blew. Julie turned to see a billow of steam rising from the approaching locomotive. She stared down the length of the train just in time to see her partner engaged in an epic sword fight with a group of cowboy bandits.

Julie contemplated what to do. Her partner could be made into mulch by those swords. While Julie thought, Beck used the distraction to her advantage. Leaping up, she grabbed the ladder on the end car just in time to hitch a ride.

Julie rolled her eyes, slid down the fake pyramid, and took after her. Rocks, dust, and Styrofoam chunks broke off and rolled down with her.

Beckensalepulledherselfuptothenarrowsidestepsofthetrainc arandthenswungaroundtolookback. With the smile of a suave escape artist, Beck waved goodbye to Julie Kingston, who was falling behind. The train went around a bend and disappeared into a tunnel, dressed as an abandoned coal mine.

Julie gauged that the track was about a quarter-mile loop. Pausing, she put her hands on her hips and looked down the tracks and then back toward the tunnel again, pondering the best course of action. Making up her mind, she turned in the opposite direction, away from the tunnel. She would cut them off at the pass.

8

The Hollywood Express

As the train came out of the dark mouth of the tunnel, all four remaining sword combatants stood at ease, pausing long enough to let their eyes grow accustomed to the sudden change in light. Upon regaining their vision, the clanging and clashing of tempered steel resumed.

ThethreeremainingbanditsbroughttheirswordsdownontoScarecrowwitharesounding

CHA – CHINK!

Even though he successfully blocked the blow, John was forced to drop to his knees to absorb the brunt of the assault, barely holding his attackers at bay.

Snarling rabidly, the leader pressed down with all of his weight and growled, "It's the end of the line for you, funny face!"

"But...," grunted Scarecrow. "We're...on... an elliptical track."

"Whatever!" the leaders snapped back. The three remaining bandit assassins briefly let up and positioned themselves. Once again, they encircled Scarecrow. As they closed in on their prey, the splintered, cracked, and dented tips of their swords gleamed like the jagged teeth of a bloodthirsty shark.

As they drew near, Scarecrow raised his shimmering sword above his head—the katakana catching light and glinting in the sun. Sensing a final strike was imminent, Scarecrow readjusted his stance to deflect their final advance better.

Giving it all they could muster, the bandit assassins leaped forward and shouted from the gut.

"Ki—Yahhh!"

Each of their swords pierced Scarecrow, who did little to resist them. The sharp blades of his attackers passed easily through him and pierced the outlaw's side. Slowly, the realization sank into their faces that they had all been skewered. Simultaneously, the villains collapsed.

Scarecrow remained motionless, his arms resting limply at his sides as he stood on top of the speeding locomotive's train car. With three samurai swords lodged in history, he resembled a ragdoll pierced by the pins of a mad Voodoo priest. Scarecrow's suit gently fluttered in the breeze as the train chugged along the tracks, giving him a rather stoic appeal.

"Oh my God!" a woman's voice cried out, horrified by the ugly sight of swords protruding from Scarecrow's torso.

Scarecrow strained his neck to see a sexy cowgirl climbing up onto the top of the train car with him. It was his idol, Kateland Rameses Beckensale.

"Does it hurt badly? "Beck asked, her voice suddenly taking on a seductively sympathetic tone.

"It looks worse than it is," Scarecrow assured her. He continued to add, "I can't feel physical pain. Emotional pain, however, is a different story."

Beck bit her lip and continued her act of seduction. "You are a poor, sensitive thing. Is there anything I can do to help make you feel better?"

"Ah, well, you're just saying that because you're a little confused right now," Scarecrow replied as politely as possible.

"If you don't mind me asking, what makes you think I'm confused?"

"Mostly the way you dress," Scarecrow informed. "You're working for the other team."

"Maybe you're right. But every story needs its villain," she retorted.

"Are you?"

"Am I what?"

"The villain?"

"I plead the fifth."

"Smart choice. Is there anything else I should be aware of?

"I don't know. Maybe? "I'm part Jewish," Beck said.

"I mean more like along the lines of anything relevant to current events."

"Then no."

"You know," Scarecrow said, eyeing Beck from head to toe, "I'm just not seeing it. "You look like an evil mastermind."

"Well, aren't you just a great big sweetheart?" Beck brushed the hair out of her eyes and looked up at him with a bewitching smile. "I may not be evil mastermind material, but to tell you a little secret, I can be a naughty girl."

John thought about that for a moment and reluctantly put it out of his mind the next.

"Well, in that case," John informed her, "I think I may have to interrogate you. You know, for concealed items."

"Frisk me, strip search me, do what you want to me. But before you do, I have a small confession to make." Beck rose onto her tiptoes and whispered into his ear, "I like to kiss the rod."

Scarecrow gulped hard and tugged at the collar of his shirt. His voice was weaker than before; he cleared his throat and said, "I mean to ask you some questions, not strip-search you."

"We can do that later," Beck replied, licking her lips. "First things first, handsome. Take my clothes off. Go ahead, search every inch of me."

"Boy, you know how to turn up the heat, don't you? "Scarecrow asked, fiddling more with his overheated collar.

"You know it," Beck said, giving her best southern drawl. Having fun toying with her new pet, Beck used her feminine wiles to distract him all the more. Unfastening the top button of her leather vest, her bosom flooded into the enlarged opening. John was unable to remove his eyes from her swelling cleavage.

Biting her bottom lip, Becks squeaked, "As you can see, I have nothing to hide."

After sliding her hands seductively down the curvature of her body, she reached over and slid them up John's wiry physique. Her left hand quickly found the handle of one of the swords still protruding from John's chest. She gently massaged the sword handle with soft, delicate motions, kissed it, and said, "You poor thing."

Meanwhile, her other hand found his and intertwined their fingers like an intimate couple. Leaning in even more, she pressed her bulging cleavage into his arm, mashing her breasts into him even harder.

Johnwatchedattentivelyassweatglideddownhersternumand aroundthehumpofherbreasts, then slowly dripped down into the valley of her cleavage. He gulped hard at the overly arousing sight.

Beck looked deep into his eyes and smiled sinfully. John gulped again. Just then, he experienced a peculiar sensation, and a strange grin spread across his face.

"What's the matter, darlin'?" she inquired, her glistening breasts pressed firmly against his body.

"I seem to have become overly stimulated by your innate attractiveness," answered Scarecrow. At that very moment, Beck's eyes met this, and together, their joint gaze panned down the length of his body to hold the massive bulge swelling in his

"Let my partner go, you psycho-f@#k-fruitcake!" Julie's voice rang out, aghast at the sight she had stumbled upon.

Startled, as if they were two teenagers caught in a make-out session behind the school bleachers, John and Beck spun around to see Julie standing at the end of the same train car.

Ignoring the strands of hair blowing in front of her eyes, Julie aimed her Sig Sauer straight at Beck and gave her most menacing glare—the kind reserved especially for back stabbing bitches and fiancé-snatching whores.

Beck, in desperation, grabbed Scarecrow from behind and pulled one of the swords out of history. This was the second time he had been made into a human shield today. Without intending to, he let out a sigh.

"Stay back, Kingston!" warned Beck, holding the blade up to John's neck.

"If you ask me," interjected Scarecrow, "I preferred the flirting."

"Sorry to disappoint, my pet. But nobody is going to lock me up. Least of all, some man-juggling thunder cu—"

"Ladies! Please, let's be civilized here. Perhaps a little less tabloid-worthy, some candy mongering, and a little more respect for one another? Love. It's what the world needs. Right now."

Pausing momentarily to think about Scarecrow's advice, both women's eyes locked, and as if electric beams of charged energy crackled between their frenzied stares, they ignored him.

Bitch, whore, whore and *bitch* were exchanged without remorse as John stood, shaking his head in dismay.

Giving it all she had, Becks suddenly shoved Scarecrow toward Julie, then immediately ran in the opposite direction. Sprinting toward the conductor's cabin at the front of the locomotive, Beck made a break for it.

Stumbling, John started to slip over the side of the train when suddenly a hand reached out and caught him in the nick of time. Julie held onto Scarecrow's arm tightly and pulled him back onto the train. "Gotcha!"

"Thanks," he replied, brushing himself off. Looking back, I noticed Julie giving him an exacting look.

"You were flirting with her, weren't you?"

"Who? Me?"

"At least I finally figured out what your weakness is."

"Beautiful women?"

"Slutty cowgirls."

"It's the boots," Scarecrow replied earnestly. "Long, silky, tan legs receding into the tight-fitting leather wrap of an elegant boot—it's like my Kryptonite."

"Funny," Julie began, "I pegged you for a breast man."

"Well, of course. Those too. I'm impartial when it comes to the female anatomy."

"Well, why don't we just call you' Ladies Love Cool Johnny '?" Pausing for a bit, Julie glanced down at the massive bulge filling the crotch of John's pants. Shutting her eyes, she exhaled and took a deep breath. After a second of contemplation, she opened her eyes and gazed up at John inquisitively.

John looked down, then back at Julie, did a slight double-take, and grinned sheepishly. Julie looked away due to the awkwardness of it all.

"I know what you must be thinking," Scarecrow informed her.

"Do you?" Julie asked earnestly.

"It's a sock," John reassured her.

"I had better be," Julie stated dryly.

John shrugged.

Although she did her best not to look interested, secretly, deep down inside, she had a burning desire to find out whether or not it was a sock. But in the end, she decided that too much knowledge might be a bad thing.

9

Risqué Business

CIRCLING THE BEND, THE TRAIN CAME OUT FROM BEHIND A thick grove of pines and made its way back down the tracks, heading straight toward the miniature Egyptian landscape. Steel squealed as the train's brakes bit down. Sparks sprayed out from under the giant serpentine machine's belly as the eighty-ninth-ton metal monstrosity screeched to a halt in front of the pyramids. Kateland Rameses Beckensale leaped from the conductor's cab and dashed back toward the sound stages.

Julie grabbed the sword from John's chest and pulled it out. "I hope you don't mind if I borrow this.

"Be my guest," John answered, dislodging the final blade from his chest before throwing it away.

Leaping down from the side of the passenger car, Julie once again engaged in hot pursuit of her suspect. Catching up to her spur-heeled rival at the Sphinx, Julie, out of breath, put her hands on her knees as she gasped for air between words. "I'm tired... of chasing you," she panted. "So what do you say we just wrap this up and you come down to answer some questions?"

Without hesitation, Becklund lunged forward, swinging her sword wildly. Evading the swipes of the blade, Julie brought her sword up, parried, and deflected the subsequent attack.

Exhausted by the iron and mouse game, the two women took big, heavy swings with their swords. Missing each other on the first two swings, they finally made contact, and their blades rang out with a CLANG! and a TWANG! as metal scraped against metal.

Hitting again, the swords ignited with sparks, and suddenly the two women locked blades and pressed themselves together. Standing nose to nose, Beck glared at Julie. "I know you think I'm crazy—but I'm not."

"Tell it to the jury," Julie said through clenched teeth. The two women broke away and continued their fight until they could barely keep the swords raised and were panting for breath. With a heavy hand and an arm, Julie let the tip of her sword rest on the ground. Sweat glistened across her face and neck. Looking down at the blade, which was nicked, dented, and worn out, Julie finally decided to discard it and toss it aside.

Beck took the opportunity to mount one last desperate attack, but Julie kicked the sword out of her rival's hands and sent it flying to the ground before she could swing. Before Beck could retrieve it, Julie swiftly pulled out her sidearm and slammed the gun into the temple of Beck's head. A resounding thwack dropped the cowgirl to the ground.

Disoriented from the blow, Beck stumbled to her feet, but before she could regain her bearings, she dropped back down to her knees. Everything was spinning.

Julie casually holstered her gun and brushed off her hands. Standing before Beck, Julie raised her fist high above her head, and with considerable irritation, she spat out one final complaint, "I've had it up to here with you."

Then, with a cheap sort of pleasure, Julie cold-cocked Beck.

THRACK!

Struggling through the darkness that filled her aching head, Beck opened her eyes to see nothing but blue sky. It was peaceful. Serene. Lying on her back, Beck concluded that taking a hit wasn't all it was cracked up to be. After all, that's what stunt doubles are for.

Beck rolled over and pushed herself up to her knees. As the ground came back into focus beneath her, she timidly touched her bloodied lip with her finger and instantly retracted her hand from the sharp sting. Cocking her head to the side, she spat crimson-stained saliva onto the dirt.

"You bitch," Beck hissed. "You mangled my face!"

"You bet your mental ass I did. Someone had to knock some sense into you! You assaulted an officer, fled from the scene of a crime, and then proceeded to flirt with said officer's partner. Leading lady or not, you had it coming."

"You never even listened to what I had to tell you, Kingston!"

Julie looked at Beck in disbelief. The whole situation was absurd. "We've already been down this road, sweetheart. Read my lips when I say, '*I don't give a flying flip, sweetheart.*'"

"Typical," Beck huffed angrily.

"I just want to know one thing. Why are you trying to kill me?"

Kateland Rameses Beckensale slowly got back up to her feet and wiped the blood from her lip with the back of her hand, grimacing from the sting.

Julie, now feeling bad for cold-cocking Beck, extended her hand outward in a gesture of peace. Beck ignored her gesture and kept her distance.

"Look, Beck, I'm sorry... but you were out of control."

"Are you going to arrest me?"

"Not if you tell me who's behind this and why," Julie answered.

Quite unexpectedly, Beck grabbed Kingston by the back of her neck, pulled her in, and gave her a big, long, profoundly penetrating French kiss.

Julie could only respond as a person with a mouthful of tongue usually does in such a situation: with a "*Mmm-phff-mmph.*"

BecksmelledthesideofJulie'sneckandranherfingersthroughJulie'shair.

"What the hell was that about?!"

Beck looked like she would do it again, and Julie reeled backward, swatting Beck's hand away.

"Seriously, what's the matter with you?"

Julie stepped back, tripped over her heels, and fell onto her ass with a hard *"Oomphf!"*

Beck slowly bent down, her hip thrusting out. She got onto all fours and crawled onto the top of Julie. Hovering over her, Beck pressed her breasts and pelvis on Julie's chest and thighs, sighing with the release of pure, adulterated pleasure.

With Beck practically lying on top of her, Julie couldn't decide, as all of them were equally awkward.

Just as Julie was about to voice her displeasure, Beck kissed her again. Julie's eyes grew wide with surprise, barely managing to get out a *"Whuh-mmm."*

To fend off Beck's sexual advances, Julie decided to push Beck away bravely. Julie's hands awkwardly groped Beck's chest, which only seemed to make Beck moan even louder.

"For God's sake!" Julie cried out in frustration.

"Don't stop!" Beck pleaded. Placing her hands on top of Julie's, Beck forced her to squeeze down even harder, aiding Julie in groping her breasts.

"Yes, don't stop," said a voice, followed by a muffled snicker and the mechanical sound of an automatic zoom lens focusing in and out; then, in rapid succession, the digital sound of a shutter lens clacked.

The two women paused and looked over to where the sound came from, only to see Scarecrow filming their little lesbian encounter with the digital camera on his smartphone. John focused on Beck straddling Julie's lap and took a few additional shots for good measure.

With a forced politeness, Julie enquired, "What are you doing, John?"

"Providing backup," he informed. "Just pretend I'm not here."

Having had enough, Julie grabbed Beck's wrists, flipped her onto her chest, and rolled on top of her, pinning her down.

"Don't move," Julie said, twisting Beck's right arm behind her back. Unbeknownst to her, Beck's and her fingers soon found their way into her bikini bottom. "You have the right to remain silent," Julie began. Just then, Beck released a deep, penetrating moan.

"You might be interested in what the other hand is doing," John informed his partner.

"Your son is helping the situation anyway," Julie said, glaring back at Scarecrow and giving him the evil eye.

"Although I speak only for myself," John interjected with a slightly condescending grin, "I find this whole turn of events rather stimulating."

"Put a sock in it!" Julie said to her partner as she roughly cuffed Beck's hands behind her back, slapping the cuffs on as hard as she could.

"Ouch!" Beck squawked in pain. "Why did you do that?"

"Don't you like it rough?" Julie asked rhetorically, pulling Beck back up to her feet.

"I do, but there's a difference between being rough and being mean."

"I'm sorry, did I interrupt your enjoyment of yourself down on the ground?"

"You can be a real bitch sometimes," Beck said with pouting lips.

"You're the b—"

"Ladies, ladies," John interrupted with a sincere urgency. Both women stopped and looked at him.

"What is it?"

"I just realized I may have been shooting in lower resolution than I wanted. Is there any chance we could reshoot some of the best takes?"

"I'm up for it," Beck said, turning towards Julie and shooting her a sensual smile.

"Oh, shut up! Both of you. And I mean it. One more peep out of you," Julie said to Beck, "and you'll be riding in the trunk." Turning toward John, she said, "And one more peek out of you, and you'll be taking the city bus back to the precinct." Then she snapped her fingers at John and held her open palm out as if to say, "Hand it over."

John popped the SD card out and handed it to her. Julie threw it down on the ground and crushed it under the heel of her foot. John watched helplessly as a perfect SD card went to waste.

Julie forcefully nudged Beck together to start walking back toward the car, and the two women continued their bickering.

Once they had made it out of earshot, a devilish smile spread across John's lips, pulling his mouth stitches so tight that they threatened to burst from their seams.

Reaching his inside coat pocket, he pulled out the SD card. Scarecrow didn't try to suppress his delighted giddiness as he flicked the SD card into the air like a coin and caught it again, smug confidence pressed onto her burlap lips.

CASEFILE:2

Sugar and Spice and All Things Vice

CLASSIFIED

10

The Sex-Files

DEAD BODIES LITTERED THE HOTEL SUITE. SPRAWLED OUT across the bed lay the cold body of Senior Californian Senator Mark Durrell. Julie Kingston took her time inspecting him, resting her hands on her hips as she ran through every possible scenario in her mind which would aid her in determining what exactly the f@#k happened here.

The senator lay on his back, staring up at the ceiling, his eyes bulging like a dead fish on dry land from some erotic asphyxiation gone horribly awry. Two naked prostitutes lay dead on either side of him. Glass mirrors with lines of cocaine cut out on them sat on the small coffee table in the middle of the room, along with a half-finished glass of red wine.

Julie surmised that the victims had probably gotten high and, in a state of ecstasy, hadn't noticed that they had accidentally taken too much. In the end, the Senator's sexual proclivities had been the death of him—a victim of his vice. "And then the gasper could gasp no more," Julie whispered as she ran over the scenario in her mind.

"Pardon?" asked Jack Wolfe, a rookie detective, returning with Julie's coffee. As Jack went to hand Julie the coffee, a forensic investigator rudely barged past and almost spilled it. Jack saved it in time and finally handed it to Julie.

"Nothing. I was talking to myself," Julie replied, taking the small paper cup of steaming black coffee. "So noob, what's your take on these little escapades gone awry?"

Brushing his hands down, Wolf looked over the scene and expounded, "Well, Detective, I'd say that the senator got what he wanted." The two girls choked him to within an inch of his life, but he bit off more than he could chew, and in a moment of passion, one of the girls inadvertently choked the life out of him. Realizing what they had done, and fearing the consensus, they tried to take an easy out, and deliberately overdosed."

"Makes sense," Julie agreed. "We could assume that the consequences of having accidentally murdered a U.S. senator weighed so heavily on their consciences that they saw no way out but to commit suicide. It's possible."

"Then again, they could have been high as kites prior to the incident and simply may not have noticed," Wolfe added, wanting to change his answer to something more plausible. "The overdoses could have simply been accidental."

"Negligent homicide followed by accidental suicide, then? Is that your final answer?"

"Yeah, I'm sticking with it."

"What about the fourth victim?" Julie asked as she and Wolf turned toward a beautiful, porcelain-skinned woman who sat at the head of the joining room of the hotel's suite. She was propped up on a leather sofa, her eyes wide open, staring vacantly at the living room. "How do you explain her?"

"She probably overdosed on the same bad batch," Detective Wolfe said, tucking his hands into his pants pockets.

Julie took a sip of the black brew and looked over at John Scarecrow, crouched before the third victim, eyeing her with a piercing gaze. "Care to enlighten him, Scary?"

John smiled to himself. He liked it when she called him Scary. Scratching his chin, John said, "The problem with the kid's theory is that nothing is as it seems. First, there's no suicide note. If this were a suicide pact, at least one of the girls would have had loved ones she'd want to inform. An accidental overdose is more plausible, but they're using top-grade drugs, so it doesn't seem likely that that bad batch slipped in. So if it wasn't an accident, it had to be something else. And the only thing I can think of is that it isn't a case of accidental manslaughter or suicide is, well, murder. This is a case of outright homicide."

"Wait a minute," Wolf said, raising his hands and gesturing for everyone to hold on. "Are you trying to tell me the senator was assassinated?"

"No," Scarecrow replied, standing back. "The senator appears to have been collateral damage."

"Okay, you lost me," Wolfe admitted, a perplexed look solidifying on his face. "I don't even see how that can be a valid inference. By all accounts, it appears like an open-and-shut case of accidental manslaughter."

"Exactly. That's the first clue that everything is not what it appears to be," Julie asserted. "The crime scene is too perfect. Everything is right in its place, leading you to that conclusion. In all my time with homicide, I've never seen a crime scene perfectly laid out. Crime scenes are always messy. It's the one thing you can count on. But this one is merely putting on the pretense of being messy."

"The question is," the Scarecrow chimed in, "why is this pristine figurine of a woman sitting alone on her little island, frozen in a moment of sadness for all eternity?" What is she looking at? Why is she here? Who is she? If you were to walk into this room here, everything would seem normal. But there she is, an oddity caught in the aftermath of a clichéd tragedy.

"Sure, it's odd. But it's not out of the realm of impossibility that she just happened to be here."

"But why is she dead?" Scarecrow said, looking over at Jack. "If she's alone over here, and the party was going on over there, why is she dead?"

"Like I said," Jack insisted, "they overdosed."

"Don't you think that if she had overdosed first, the others would not have noticed and avoided the bad drugs? Or if they overdosed first, she would have either called 911 or fled the scene of the crime? Why hang around and take the same bad drugs only for housekeeping to stumble upon this whole tragic mess after the fact?"

"You see, rookie, "Julie began as she walked over to the woman sprawled on the bed. "There's a blonde and an Asian girl here next to the senator. The blonde is draped over the bed, face down, and the Asian girl is lying flat on her back, staring up at the ceiling with a trickle of dried blood under her nose. But if you look closer, Detective, what do you see?"

"Just your standard fare hookers, ma'am."

"This is a Yin and Yang combo-platter," Julie informed him. "East meets West meets cock'n'balls. It's a standard package for those home-grown, blue-collar American boys who have grown up on a steady supply of white bread but may want to feel a little bit daring and try some whole wheat instead. What you need to keep in mind is the fact that the Asian is out of place."

"How so, Lieutenant?"

"Senator Durrell was a homophobe and a racist," Julie added. "Republican big shots like him almost always are. So, how do you explain a homophobic racist being caught up in a bi-racial, bi-sexual sex orgy?"

"If the senator was a racist and a homophobe, it's not a stretch of the imagination that he was also a hypocrite. Maybe he had a white-male superiority complex and wanted to play out some sadistic fantasy of dominating a non-white girl."

"You seem to be forgetting that he was the gasper. In other words, he wasn't the sadist type, he was the masochist type," John reminded Jack. "So, you see, this is how we know the Asian was out of place."

"Makes sense," Jack said, rubbing his chin.

"Which brings us back to this girl." Looking over at Jack, she informed, "Okay, hotshot. This is your last chance to provide us with a working theory.

"Perhaps..." Jack said, drawing out his sentence as he thought aloud. "Perhaps she's the killer?"

Julie almost spit out the other coffee, then took a hard gulp and looked at Jack with widened eyes. Once she regained her composure, her eyes narrowed into her trademark hard-boiled, Remington-steel gaze.

"Ahman!" Wolf said, throwing up his arms.

"That's right, genius. Bagels for a week."

Scarecrow leaned over and whispered into Julie's ear, "And he was doing so well, too."

Grabbing Detective Wolfe by the tie, Julie led him over to the porcelain-skinned blonde. "What is she?"

"I don't follow."

"She's a third party?" Scarecrow added.

"Yeah, so?"

Julie sighed. "We know the senator is a racist, so we have to account for the Asian girl. The only way to do that is to assume he ordered two girls, but one of them was Asian, the senator called another service to have a different girl brought up."

"Or he had someone else get another girl for him," Scarecrow added."

"Okay, I'm following you guys so far."

"So why is the Asian girl still here? If she replaced her, why didn't she leave?"

Jack Wolfe nodded in the affirmative but quickly switched to a negative, "I have no idea."

"Because the second girl was late getting here," Julie stated. "If she had arrived on time, the Asian would have been dismissed. But it still takes two women to cater to the senator's needs. One to choke a man as large as the senator, and the other to do the sexual favors. If you were putting your life in the hands of a racist, would you give that privilege to the white girl or the ethnic girl who you despise and who despises you back?"

"Oh, I see what you're getting at," Wolfe said, scratching the back of his head. Another pushy forensics investigator pushed by, shoving Wolfe out of the way. Wolfe ignored him and continued to focus on figuring out the riddle. "So the senator, assuming that if anything went wrong, didn't want to die at the hands of a person of ethnicity due to his racial biases. But he would have no problem allowing her the 'honor' of pleasuring him, the white master, even as a submissive little scalawag."

"Exactly," Julie said, standing before the mysterious woman and gazing at her contemplatively, taking another sip of her coffee.

"She has hauntingly attractive eyes," Scarecrow interjected.

"Whoever she was," Julie added, "she's not your stereotypical pimp-battered crack whore. She has no marks of any kind, which means she most likely worked for a professional escort service. Some places ensure their girls are well cared for."

"So what's your theory, Lieutenant?" Wolfe inquired, taking out a pen and pad to take notes. "I'm dying to know."

"The fourth girl killed him."

"I have to ask," Wolf said, raising his eyebrow in curiosity, "what makes you so certain there was a mysterious fourth girl?"

Julie pointed back toward the senator and the two hookers lying on the bed with him. "Because the senator wanted two girls. You can't have a kinky threesome without two girls, now, can you?"

"You see," John said, sweeping his gloved hand across the crime scene. "We've been assuming this whole time that the two prostitutes on the bed arrived first."

"Oh, now I get it," Jack Wolfe chirped excitedly. "You're saying that he ordered two girls, but they were late, so he lost his patience with his aide's lack of experience in dealing with such delicate matters. He picked up two more for himself from right off the street.

"Go on," Julie encouraged.

Tapping the syringe full of pentothal, Wolfe continued, "So the evening's activities commenced, and halfway into the orgy, the late woman arrives." Only now are they incensed because they might not get paid, so things escalate as they often do, and then somebody cries foul play. The only question is, why would the fourth girl kill her colleague? That doesn't make any sense."

"That's the question, isn't it?" Julie agreed. "We must assume this woman is being singled out."

Just then, an officer in blue stepped up to Scarecrow, whispered something in his ear, and handed him a slip of paper. John looked down and smiled.

"What is it?" Wolf asked.

Holding up the paper slip, Scarecrow said, "They caught up with the senator's aide. As it turns out, he did order two call girls. He was escorting them to the room when he found the senator in the middle of a happy ending. After that, he headed to the bar to try to drink himself into a stupor and erase the memory of everything he'd just seen.

"Does it say all that on that slip of paper, then?" Julie asked, her green eyes narrowing, and a slight smirk spreading across her face.

John winked at her, but it was clear that Wolfe was more than a little confused. Wolfe just looked back, and for that, he tapped rhythmically on his notepad.

You're just messing with me. You already questioned the aide, didn't you?"

Julie laughed and slapped Wolfe on the back. "It's called detective work. You might want to try it sometime." With that, she turned and exited the hotel suite.

"Well, rookie, look on the bright side. Now, we must track down the escort service and interview some pretty ladies."

"Do you think she hates my guts?"

"Who? Lieutenant Kingston?"

"I mean, how are you not terrified of her?"

"Because," John informed, his voice deepening and growing raspy. She's not the one you should be worried about. I am." Making the gesture of pointing at his own eyes, his fingers tracking until they latched onto Wolfe's, he made it crystal clear that he was watching him. With that, John Scarecrow slowly backed away for dramatic effect and slipped out the door.

Jack Wolfe turned back around and stood for a while, tapping the pen on the pad and looking at the sad expression on the girl's face. Suddenly, he heard a faint voice whisper, "Don't forget the bagels."

Turning around, Jack found himself face-to-face with Scarecrow's wholly inhuman face.

"Holy mother of pearl!" Jack squealed, completely frightened out of his wits. "Can't you sneak up on me like that? Some days, being the rookie just wasn't any fun. It was a lot like being the bottom rung on a ladder. You were always the first one everybody stepped on to get where they wanted.

John Scarecrow repeated his gesture, eyeing Jack suspiciously. Again, he slowly backed away. With that, Scarecrow disappeared around the corner once more.

11

All in a Day's Work

CITY HALL IN DOWNTOWN L.A. GLEAMED IN THE MIDDAY sun. The white monolith shone like a beacon of inspiration to the people of the City of Angels. At least that's the impression Julie got as she climbed the stairs and walked underneath the Parthenon-like pillars on her way to the district attorney's office.

Julie stood in the hall, waiting outside the DA's office, nervously pacing back and forth. Julie rarely got worked up about anything, but if something truly made her uneasy, it was having to go toe-to-toe with the DA. She knew that whenever she was called into the office, it was because she'd become an insurance liability to the city and a huge legal hassle, so it was no wonder the DA, Megan Powers, never seemed all that pleased to meet with her.

The past year has been a whirlwind of one crazy event after. First was the circus, the incident with the mad clown, and the subsequent hot-air balloon chase. It didn't matter that the event leading up to the aggravatingly slow chase involved the man wearing nothing but underwear.

Then there was the snake-man assassin, who poisoned his victims with snake venom. It took her darn near a week to figure out why hikers were entering the park only to be discovered dead somewhere along the trail. Only with the toxicology report was she able to figure out that they had all died of snake venom, despite the absence of bite marks.

Julie had just been in the most enormous shootouts since Prohibition, and the new DA sought to establish a name for herself, meaning she intended to play hardball. Julie knew she would receive mostly criticism and slight to no support from Powers.

Itdidn'thelpmattersthatJuliehadfastbecomethecity'scelebrity super-copeither. She was known for her volatile personality and temper, which were hotter than those of a jalapeno.

It was no secret what the rest of the precinct thought of her, and she knew that they all called her "Hot Tamale" behind her back. Although she made a fuss about it whenever somebody used it with her, she secretly liked it.

The paparazzi seemed to be waiting for her to do something wild and reckless everywhere she went. She had once known a paparazzi in her groin for flashing unsolicited shots of her coming out of a trail, for which she was being sued for reckless endangerment of the whole city of L.A. When the idiot stepped in front of her, cutting her off and asking when her next big mistake would make headlines, she simply replied, "How about a scoop?"

She didn't know what it was, but she had the unfortunate habit of making the evening news more often than most celebrities. Just this year, she'd started receiving invitations to official celebrity functions, which she tried to maintain a positive public relations image for the city's law enforcement. It seemed to work for the most part.

The only problem with being the new face of justice, however, was that the bad guys were all gunning for her, and the city had to take out an extra insurance policy on her to cover the cost of the destruction that she often left in the wake of her unique style of law enforcement.

But at the end of the day, every single one of her choices, reckless or not, was justified. To her, it didn't matter what everyone else thought. It was likely the wrong thing to do if she couldn't explain something to herself. And of course, she did her best to work within the confines of the law. She would have been canned a long time ago if she hadn't. It was just a few days; her effort was lacking.

MeganPowers'secretaryledJuliethroughthelargeofficedoors andgesturedforJulietotakeaseatinfrontofherdesk. The tall bookshelves built into the walls, the leather furniture, and the rich colors of the burgundy walls and navy carpet made the room seem more regal somehow, more like the Oval Office than a regular office. Legal books lined the shelves on one side, and two burgundy leather chairs complemented the antique mahogany desk.

A few minutes later, Power entered through a side door of the office with a folder of paperwork; she looked over the wintered-colored eyeglass frames she wore and smiled at Julie.

"Sorry to keep you waiting, "Megan said as she sat at the desk. She quickly finished signing her name to some important documents and then looked up at Julie with a look that seemed as though she were summing her up.

Old Glory dangled majestically behind Powers, stars and stripes contrasting with her charcoal-gray suit, lending her an air of authority. Julie smiled politely and waited for Powers to speak first.

"You're probably interested in why I called you in here?"

"I can't take a guess," Julie responded, her otherwise cheerful smile fading into an anxious grin.

The mayor is breathing down my neck to improve our public relations image for conducting business. This isn't the Wild West anymore; it's the twenty-first century, and I have it on good authority that the taxpayers of L.A. do not appreciate the mess created by reckless law enforcement agents.

"If you read my report..." Julie began.

"I've read it," Powers interrupted, as she tossed a file on the desk before Julie. "And no surprise here, it's full of reckless stubbornness."

Julie bit her bottom lip but couldn't find anything worthwhile to say in her defense. There was no denying the facts.

"Although I commend you on apprehending the offenders who caused today's incident, the fact is, you lucked out. If there had been one, just one civilian casualty, you would have been handed your job."

"I get that, but..."

"Let me finish," Powers asserted. Julie bit her tongue. "Two of the thugs you assaulted are pressing charges against the city for cruel and unusual punishment, police harassment, police brutality, and failure to read them their Miranda rights properly."

"What?" Julie chirped in annoyance. "That's total bullshit. They opened fire with illegal, fully automatic weapons in public and endangered civilian lives. I did what had to be done."

Powers raised her hand and stopped Julie there. "Never mind the charges. They won't stick. The point is, you can't continue to be the maverick out there. It's costing the city too much, and the only reason the mayor still allows you to keep your job is due to the city's current fascination with your celebrity status. But don't think your luck will last because it won't."

Feeling uncomfortable, Julie shuffled in her seat, but it didn't help.

"Look, Kingston, I know it doesn't sound like it, but I'm fully on your side here." But you're walking on eggshells as it is. One more slip-up, and you'll be working traffic. Even so, you're still one of the city's finest, and just like I need my best lawyers working the tough criminal cases, the city needs its best protectors working out there in the nightmare of reality that we call our lives."

Meg took off her glasses, huffed some steamy breath onto them, and polished them off with a cloth she had tucked inside her jacket. She sighed, put the glasses back on, and continued her lecture.

"Since everyone I've spoken with seems to think you're the best detective the city has to offer, I'm afraid we need to incur the cost of the damages. But I'm asking you as a favor, please, cool your jets. And for God's sake, Kingston, stop trying to get yourself killed."

"I'll do my best, ma'am."

"I would expect nothing less. So, here's the deal. I need you out there to catch the bad guys so I can prosecute them and put them behind bars where they belong. So I went ahead and pulled a few strings and called in some old favors. The Chief of Police had no qualms about my request, so as of today, you're being promoted to police lieutenant."

Julie cocked her head slightly and brushed a tuft of her hair behind her ear. Eyeing Powers suspiciously, she asked, "A promotion? Are you serious?"

"Dead serious."

"I don't believe it."

"As I said, you're the best investigator we have. We need the best training for the next generation of detectives. It's as simple as that. To do that, you must be able to provide leadership and oversee the investigations personally.

AwidesmilestretchedacrossJulie'smouthassheflashedherpearlywhites. Standing up, she saluted Powers. "Well, then, in the famous words of Alecia Beth Moore, let's get this party started."

SETTING A BOX OF HER PERSONAL ITEMS ON HER NEW desk, Julie paused to look around at the excellent square footage of her new corner office. It had a glass wall to look over the detectives. Captain Greenblatte's office was the next one over, and behind her new digs was the break room. She couldn't have asked for a better spot—the perfect distance for feeding her ungodly coffee addiction.

Turning toward the back wall, she noted that the empty bookshelf and cabinets were handcrafted and nicely integrated into the wall. On the floor, five cardboard file boxes were filled with freshly printed curriculum vitae, each accompanied by a personal profile of a potential detective candidate. Julie sighed, a drawn-out sound, dreading the thought of reviewing a monotonous pile of over-qualified, overly confident resumes from every supercop in the city. The captain wanted her recommendations by the end of the week.

Lounging in her office, Julie put her feet upon her desk. Looking up, she watched John Scarecrow enter the room holding two manila envelopes. He handed Julie one of them, and she reached in and pulled out a tabloid-sized sheet. Placing it on the desk, she looked fondly at it.

"Since we can no longer be formal partners, I thought I'd give you this parting gift."

"That's considerate of you, John," she said, holding up the photograph for John to see. "But this is a nude glamor shot of Kateland Rameses Beckensale."

Embarrassed, John quickly retrieved the picture, tucked it back into the first envelope, and then handed her the other envelope.

Julie carefully opened the new envelope and pulled out a small plastic bag containing a silver chain threaded through a silver bullet. Beautifully etched on the side of the bullet casing was the inscription *rūhiustise*.

"It's Old English for 'rough justice,'" John informed her. Julie slid the necklace around her neck and continued to admire its simple beauty.

"It's gorgeous. Just one question though: Why is a silver bullet?"

"The silver bullet represents a simple and seemingly magical solution to a complicated problem. It also represents the only expedient way to kill a werewolf—an entity of pure evil. Altogether, these qualities seem to sum up your form of justice quite nicely: simple, expedient, and occasionally rough."

Julie let the necklace slide down between her breasts, where it rested comfortably between her ample cleavage. Looking back at Scarecrow, she smiled. "Scary, this is the best gift anyone has ever given me. I'm flattered. I honestly don't know what to say."

"Speechless is good," he said, satisfied that his gift was well received. Before leaving her office, he gave her a simple two-finger salute and was off.

"Wait a moment," Julie beckoned, catching him before he disappeared out of sight.

John stopped, turned on his heel, and leaned in, smiling sheepishly.

Julie pointed at the other envelope under his arm. "I want you to frame that photo of Beck and put it on my wall."

A surprised expression crossed John's face. He glanced up at the wall and asked, "You want to hang a nude glamour shot of a celebrity next to the Declaration of Independence?"

"Would it be the America you and I love if I couldn't?" Julie questioned.

"I suppose not," John chuckled, and he was off again. This time, on a mission to find the perfect frame for the ideal celebrity.

Julie was known as a loose cannon, the sort of woman who had a short fuse and a loud boom, and her precinct nickname of "Hot Tamale" was a dead giveaway that she always meant business. This gave her a certain amount of leeway. She could get away with a tasteful nude glamour shot in her office without anyone ever questioning her on it. If they did, she'd ramp up the crazy and make them leave feeling that it wasn't worth the bother.

Suddenly, there was knocking on Julie's glass door. Captain Greenblatt poked his head in and said, "I just wanted to say congratulations on your promotion, Lieutenant Kingston."

"Thanks, captain, my captain."

The captain waved a cordial goodbye and continued down the hall. Julie sat back in her new desk when suddenly, the captain poked his head back into the room. "Almost forgot. Coroner's report is ready."

"Thanks for the update," Julie said.

"Also, the Fed will send their liaison, Special Agent Jersey Blair, to oversee the Senator Durrell case. I want you to act according to protocol and avoid causing unnecessary trouble. Do I make myself clear?"

"Understood," Julie answered.

"Good," Greenblatt said. But instead of leaving, he hovered in the doorway as if he had something else he wanted to say.

Julie watched him hem and haw, as if he couldn't quite remember it or didn't want to. Either way, he soon brushed it aside, making the same sweeping gesture with his hand.

"What is it?" Julie asked. "Something bothering you?"

"Oh, what? No, it's nothing important."

"Go ahead, Captain. You can tell me."

"It's just that if anything were to happen to me, God forbid, you'd be next in command."

Shooting him a big wink, Julie just smiled at him. And the captain did a double-take and then quickly marched off in agitation.

Julie could sense he was disturbed by the fact that the most volatile and dangerous policewoman on the force was next in command. However, as far as she was concerned, Greenblatt had nothing to worry about. Julie felt she was much more effective in the field. Being a plain clothes officer working on homicides was much more appealing than being a pencil pusher and having the unbearable hassle of managing an entire precinct.

12

The Devil Is in Her Kiss

SLIDING BETWEEN JANE DOE'S BREASTS, THE RAZOR-SHARP scalpels sliced into her cold sternum. Dr. Jean Paul Baudrillard, the coroner, was an elderly man with white, wispy hair and a four-day-old grizzle on his chin. A cigarette with an ever-growing trail of ash dangled from his mouth, having made the incision. Some ash broke off and fell onto the body, which Baudrillard promptly brushed away with the back of his hand before continuing the autopsy as if nothing had happened.

"Should you be smoking in here?" Scarecrow asked with concern, viewing the autopsy from the other side of the table. He felt a little perturbed at the lack of respect for the dead and crossed his straw-stuffed arms in disapproval.

Dr. Baudrillard looked up at Scarecrow, ever so subtly, gazing at him beyond the burning ember of his half-smoked cigarette. Ironically, an anti-smoking sign is on the wall. With a cold sort of bedside manner, he assured his onlooker not to worry.

"It's not like she's worried about second-hand smoke, cuz if you'll observe," Baudrillard looked down at the deceased prostitute, "she's already dead."

"I merely meant it seems a little bit disrespectful to show such disregard for the dead."

"What do the dead care if I smoke over their rotting corpses?" the doctor asked, shooting John a cold glance from under a silvery lining of bushy, furrowed eyebrows.

Scarecrow paused, then answered, "It seems disrespectful, at least to those who may have cared for the person while they were alive."

"Well, they're not alive now, are they?" Baudrillard grumbled. "Best they deal with that fact and begin the process of healing. There's no need to live in the past."

"No, I guess not," John replied with a sigh. A sad look came over Scarecrow's face, which Baudrillard couldn't help but catch out of the corner of his eye as he was about to continue with his blade. He let out a long, drawn-out sigh and looked back up at Scarecrow.

"If it will ease your conscience, Detective, you can ask the deceased victim's you can ask the deceased victim's loved ones yourself whether or not they mind depriving an old man of his disgusting habit—a habit forged from years of stress, overwork, and little pay as a slave away for endless hours in the company of death so that they might find answers that would console the bereaved. Answers that let them have closure so that they can finally find peace and let the dead rest in peace."

"Well, when you put it that way..."

"You know, I'm glad we had this little talk," Baudrillard groaned, clearing his throat. "Now, if you don't mind, I'd like to get started."

Scarecrow stood to the back wall, as far away from the wafting smoke as possible, and continued to observe the procedure.

Baudrillard put out his dwindling cigarette in the basin of a nearby bedpan that rested on a cart. John nodded, realizing that was what the bedpan was for, since it made relatively little sense for the dead to have use of a bedpan.

"Instead of wagging your chin like a bobblehead," interjected the doctor, "why don't you grab a fresh pack of smokes out of my inside jacket pocket for me?"

Scarecrow proceeded to reach into the jacket and pull out a pack of Marlboro Reds while the doctor opened the sternum of the deceased victim, slid in a clamp, and opened her chest cavity until her heart was in broad view.

Scarecrow couldn't help but feel awkward as he watched the doctor slide his hands into her chest and skillfully remove her heart.

Baudrillard held up the heart as if he were offering it to Scarecrow, then scowled. "Where's my damn cigarette?"

Scarecrow tore open the packaging and tapped on the box, allowing a single cigarette to rise up out of the package, then held it toward the doctor, who leaned over the dead body to fetch the extended cigarette with his lips.

"Do you ever find it sad?" Scarecrow found himself asking without intending to start a conversation, "That someone's so beautiful should die so tragically?"

"I find it sad," grumbled Baudrillard, "that people like you must ask such questions in the first place. As if the preciousness of life wasn't already precious enough."

Motioning with his head, Baudrillard said curtly, "There should be a light in the right-hand side pocket."

Scarecrow searched through the large jacket pocket until he found a metal object and pulled out a Zippo lighter. He was about to hand it to the doctor, but suddenly froze as he looked fearfully at it.

"What are you waiting for?" Baudrillard frowned, the unlit cigarette dangling on his bottom lip.

"You see," Scarecrow began, an unmistakable hint of nervous fear in his voice, "fire and I don't tend to get along well."

"I'm not asking you to swallow a flaming sword here," Baudrillard quipped. Holding up blood-stained latex gloves, Baudrillard said, "All I'm asking for is a damn light."

Scarecrow cupped his leather-protected hand around the cigarette lighter and lit up the doctor's cigarette. Once the smoke began to rise, Scarecrow quickly clamped the metal lid shut and hopped back, slowly making his way to the back wall.

Viewing the porcelain-white skin of their Jane Doe, Scarecrow felt the urge to say something. "The Japanese believe life is a lot like the blooming of the cherry blossoms, called Sakura. Our lives are like cherry blossoms: radiant yet short-lived, quickly fading into the season and ultimately disappearing. Some may find it sad, others may see it as sanguine. I suppose it's a little of both. But that's life."

Baudrillard paused for a moment, letting the thought linger, and almost began to smile—almost. Relapsing back into his grumpy old self, the doctor said, "Now, if you don't mind, Aristotle, I'd like to get back to my job."

JERSEY BLAIR, A TALL BLONDE WITH SHORT, BOBBED HAIR and long legs, wore a short black skirt and cut in front of Julie, edging into the morgue first. Julie rolled her eyes in exasperation and followed her. One thing was for sure: Feds were always the same. By the book and on time.

Stepping up to the body on the table, Jersey brushed her black blazer down, smoothing out the wrinkles, and asked, "What do we have here?"

Dr. Baudrillard put out his cigarette in the nearby bedpan and grumbled, "What does it look like? It's a goddamn dead body."

Julie smiled. "You'll have to pardon Special Agent Blair," she said. "She's with the FBI."

Thedoctor'sfaceremainedunimpressedashereachedoverand grabbedthechartontheendoftheexamtable, then handed it to Special Agent Blair without saying a single word. Jersey inspected the report but couldn't make heads or tails of it. She quickly handed the chart off to Juliet to inspect.

Baudrillard peeled off the crimson-splotched latex gloves and threw them in a nearby dustbin. While Julie reviewed the chart, he walked to the sink and washed his hands with special sanitizing soap. After washing, Baudrillard pulled another pack of smokes out of his jacket and tapped on the pack until the tip of a fresh cigarette budded, then kissed it up with his lips. Pulling out a gold lighter, he held it up to his mouth, but Julie spoke out just as he was about to light up.

"Crotalase?" Her eyes were as big as saucers. She recognized the MO, but she couldn't believe he was back. For starters, she knew that the perpetrator responsible for the string of hikers' deaths was serving time in California's state penitentiary. This had to be something new, which worried her.

Looking at the doctor blankly, Jersey asked, "What is Crotalase?"

Baudrillard ignored Jersey's question and addressed Julie instead. "Not only that, but over seven hundred milligrams with a toxicity of LD-50, which would lead to a lethal neurotoxicity, causing respiratory failure and tachycardia."

"C. adamanteus has a high yield and toxicity."

"C. Adamanteus fits," the doctor replied. "But so do a handful of vipers and a few types of cobra."

"Snakes? Are we talking about venom?" inquired Blair, feeling worsted by Julie's intellectual performance. "So you're saying he died of a snakebite?"

"No," growled the doctor, impatient as usual. He continued with his diagnosis. "I think he has all the pathophysiological signs of having died of snake toxins except for one small problem."

Julierememberedherexaminationofthebodyatthecrimescen eearlierandquicklyfilledintherest. "Except for the fact that there is no snake bite."

"There's not a mark on this body," Baudrillard informed. "But check this out," he said, grabbing the deceased victim's bottom lip. He pulled it back and revealed a tenderized area. "At first, I didn't make anything of it. There's nothing unusual about a woman inheriting work to show signs of tenderness from, how shall I put it, intense foreplay. But then I decided to swab the area anyway."

Once again, Julie picked up the clues. "Oral transmission of the venom?"

"Exactly," Baudrillard replied, finally lighting up. He then took his cigarette between his fingers, took a deep drag, and blew out a haze of smoke.

"How is this even possible?" Special Agent Blair inquired. "That would mean whoever poisoned her would have to have poisoned themselves first? It doesn't make any sense."

"That's why they call it a mystery," Julie stated, her edgy grin and a dash of sarcasm evident.

Jersey made a sour face at Julie and was about to come back with a sarcastic quip when a hitherto unheard voice announced from the back corner of the room.

"A snake-man!"

Startled, Jersey Blair screamed in fright. Spinning around, she saw a living, walking, talking scarecrow gazing at her with a giant grin on his face. She screamed again.

BaudrillardwincedfromalltheshriekingandeyedJerseyasifhe wasquietlyjudgingher.Which was.

"What the hell is that? "Jersey demanded to know.

"It's a scarecrow," replied Dr. Baudrillard with the clinical dryness of an astute diagnostician.

"Are you sure you're qualified for this job?" Julie asked Jersey in a snide tone. Raggedy-looking rag doll with a burlap sack for a face. You don't have to be Sherlock Holmes to determine what it is."

John stood, grinning at Jersey without saying a word, which made her even more uncomfortable. Turning around to see the scarecrow, Jersey suddenly found him standing directly in front of her face. The surprise of his sudden proximity elicited another scream from her.

"For God's sake, don't do that!" Jersey Blair exclaimed.

"Many pardons," John said in his most sincere tone.

"Goon," Julie said, looking at her partner, John Scarecrow. "You were saying something about a snake-man?"

"Yes, well, if she has no punctures of any kind, then the only reasonable explanation is that she kissed something immune to the venom."

"Are you suggesting making out with a mongoose?" Jersey asked with a half-laugh, amusing only herself.

"No, that would be ridiculous," Scarecrow replied. "But once you eliminate the impossible, whatever remains, no matter how improbable, must be the truth."

Growing impatient, Jersey got to the point and asked, "Well, I say a snake-man is pretty damn improbable, don't you think?"

"Yes," Scarecrow answered. "But not impossible."

Jersey laughed out loud, then brushed her golden bangs away from her eyes and gazed curiously at John Scarecrow for a moment. John suddenly became aware of her intense stare and became fidgety.

"Okay," Jersey said, turning to face Julie. "Herbert George here thinks we have a crazed snake-man on the loose. What does your super intellect tell you, Lieutenant Kingston?"

"Well, Special Agent Blair, my intellect tells me we can't rule out the possibility, no matter how far-fetched it may seem. Not when all the evidence suggests it, and all the other possibilities are exceedingly more absurd. Therefore, we follow the evidence and see where it leads. You know, like real detectives."

Jersey finally had had enough of Julie's snide remarks and stormed out through the swinging doors of the morgue. Julie turned toward the boys, winked at them, and followed her.

Scarecrow looked over at Dr. Baudrillard, who, without returning his glance, grabbed his jacket off the rack and pushed past the swinging doors as he made his way out into the hall.

Scarecrow followed the doctor and stopped beside him in front of the elevator. As the doctor hit the button to go up, he looked at Scarecrow from under his furrowed brow and, in his trademark brusque tone, asked, "Is there something I can help you with, Detective?"

Curious about where the doctor was going, Scarecrow asked, "So where are you headed?"

"Cigarette break," Baudrillard replied in all seriousness.

13

Provocation

JOHN SCARECROW RETURNED TO JULIE'S OFFICE. GLANCING up at the newly displayed photo of Beckensale next to the Declaration of Independence, he pulled the folder out from under his arm and handed it to Julie.

"You'll be most interested in page thirteen," John informed her. Once Julie had flipped to the appropriate page, John continued the briefing. "As you can see, in the past two months, seven call girls have either gone missing or turned up dead. All of them have worked for the madam, Ms. Mulholland Monroe. The interesting thing is that the girls are not random abductions."

Julie continued to read along as she spoke. "There's a pattern?"

"Not just any old pattern either," John continued. "The girls have an association, not just with Senator Durrell but also with a specific date on which they met him. For the past five years, they have always met on Memorial Day weekend and always in Vegas, for obvious reasons."

"What happens in Vegas stays in Vegas."

"Exactly. But five years ago, the Miss Universe Beauty Pageant booked all the hotel reservations, and the girls' meeting was relocated to L.A. That's where the first girl was found dead. According to the coroner's report, it was listed as an accidental suicide."

"That's a crock. It's clear now that the coroner was paid to falsify the report. Blame the whore for some obscure paraphilia, the senator's record remains clean instead of having to take the rap for manslaughter. Do we know who he was?"

John fiddled with his tie. "That's where it gets interesting. I'll give you three guesses he could have met with."

"Kateland Rameses Beckensale?"

"I knew whose name would come up first, but it wasn't there."

"Really? Not her? Well, there's a first time for everything."

"Have any other guesses?"

"Not a clue."

"The girl's name, according to the agency's registry, was Tiffany Blair."

Do you mean anything concerning Jersey Blair?

"I checked the autopsy report," Scarecrow said as he leaned up against her desk, "and found that she was the only girl who died of causes other than being poisoned. It seems strangulation was involved. That, along with the name thing, got me curious.

So, I sent her genetic profile to me, and, as you might have guessed, it revealed that she has sisters.

Julieleanedbackinherdeskandtookinadeepbreathassheconte mplatedwhattodonext.John watched her think.

"John," she said, "I need you to find out everything that happened between Senator Durrell and Tiffany Blair five years ago. I have a hunch that you've just uncovered our motive. Also, could you please provide me with the significance of that date?

John offered a silent salute in response to Julie's orders.

"In the meantime," Julie added, retrieving her jacket from the coat rack, "I'm going to go interview Ms. Mulholland Monroe, since she's the dealer, not to mention the best lead we've."

"I beg your pardon?" Scarecrow inquired, not following Julie's analogy. "Dealer?"

"She's the madam. She whores out girls and deals them, like a deck of cards, to the high rollers. It's the only explanation for why she'd still be alive."

Slapping his forehead, John groaned.

"What is it?" Julie asked.

"It might be too late to mention this, but about that interview, Jersey Blair said she'd handle it."

"What do you mean, 'handle it?'" Julie asked, irritated.

"Well, you know, the whole senator dying thing falls under the jurisdiction of the FBI, so she said she was headed out to Beverly Hills to talk to Ms. Mulholland Monroe about the senator's numerous affairs personally. She left about fifteen minutes ago."

"Dammit," Julie cursed, checking her watch. "If she's out for revenge for the death of her little sister, we may have just handed her the final victim."

14

Glamor and Deception

SQUEALING TO A HALT, THE GREY CHEVY CAMARO RUDELY cut off the blue Carrera GT, which was pulling into the driveway of a large mansion in Beverly Hills. Julie stepped out of the car only to get an earful.

"What the bloody hell, Lieutenant? You cut me off!"

"Special Agent Blair, haven't you ever heard the saying, "the early bird catches the worm "?"

"Yes. But as I recall," Jersey said, thumbing her chest, "this bird has jurisdiction here."

"True, you have jurisdiction over the senator's case, but as you will recall, several other homicides took place as well. Homicides involving nice young girls who have all worked for Ms. Mulholland Monroe at one time or another."

Julie Kingston and Jersey Blair walked briskly side by side up the front steps as if it were a race to see who would get to the door first, but Jersey edged Julie out and was able to ring the doorbell before her rival. Not being one to admit defeat easily,

Julie rang the bell again just for good measure. Jersey merely sighed and rolled her eyes in response to Julie's overly competitive show of pigheadedness.

Soon enough, the intercom came on, and a woman's voice, heavily accented with Spanish inflections, asked, "Whose is it?"

"It's Special Agent Blair of the FBI and Lieutenant Kingston of the L.A.P.D.," Jersey stated. "We have an appointment with Ms. Mulholland Monroe."

"Just a minute, please."

After a few moments, the large doors of the mansion swung open, and a stout Mexican American housekeeper with cherub-like arms, wearing an apron, motioned for them to enter. Madam is out back on the patio sunbathing. Please follow."

The passageway through the foyer opened into a larger living room with a fireplace so big you could walk into it. Ornate paintings hung on the walls encased in golden frames, and the furniture consisted of deep burgundy sofas and matching chairs, all embroidered with gold thread and certainly as lavish as the rest.

Above the fireplace were three black-and-white glamour photos of the leading actress, Kateland Rameses Beckensale. Shaking her head in dismay, Julie followed Jersey, who, in turn, followed the maid through the living area and out onto the back patio through sliding glass doors.

Walking along the pool's edge, Julie saw the long, tan legs of Ms. Mulholland Monroe lounging on a beach chair by the pool. Yet the chair's angle obscured her face, and a large sun umbrella provided additional shade.

"Excuse me, ma'am, but are you Ms. Monroe by any chance?" Jersey inquired.

Looking back over her shoulder, Julie jerked her thumb toward the house and said, "I'm sorry, but I have to ask, are you a fan of low-quality, B-rated Hollywood rubbish, or do you just like Kate Beckinsale's outfits?"

Ms. Monroe threw her cream latte over the edge of her chair and sat up to properly greet guests. "I'm a huge fan of Beckinsale's," the woman said grandly. "Considering they're mine."

Julie's head snapped back around to look at a familiar face. "*You?!*"

Jersey glanced at both women in surprise. "You two know each other?"

"It's a long story," Julie grumbled. "Besides," she continued, turning back to address Beck, "only you would be narcissistic enough to decorate your own home with pictures of yourself!"

"Figures," Beck replied in turn, "that the holier-than-thou Julie Kingston would find problems with being confident in one's accomplishments."

"What? That's not even..." Julie's. With a dismayed gasp, she continued, "Being beautiful is not an accomplishment! It's goddamn random genetics."

"You wouldn't understand," Beck said, brushing aside Julie's comment. "Keeping up appearances isn't easy."

Interrupting the rhythm of both women's perfectly in-tune bickering, Jersey Blair let out an obnoxiously loud sigh just to let everyone know she was impatiently waiting for them to wrap things up.

"Never mind, what the hell are you running a brothel for? "Julie inquired.

"You've got to be kidding me," Beck said as she brushed her hair back and turned her nose up at Julie as if to deny all allegations of prostitution. "I'm a legitimate businesswoman."

Julie raised her voice. "In case you didn't know this, procuring people for sex in the state of California is illegal."

"And in case you didn't know, I'm not running a brothel. It's a call service for assisted dating and relationship consolidation."

"What?! Assisted dating? Relationship consolidation? Admit it, you're just an over-glorified pimp with tits!" Julie nudged Jersey's arm. "Come on, you tell her."

Not wanting to enable her, Jersey Blair looked at Julie blankly. "You must be thinking of your other partner. You know, the one who cares. Now, if you two are done bickering?"

JulieraisedherhandandmotionedforJerseytoholdherhorsesf oramoment.Jerseyhuffed and stepped back, realizing it would be useless to persist.

"So how the hell do you and your courtesans get tied up with the assassination of a U.S. senator?"

"We prefer relationship consultants," Beck informed them, motioning for them to fetch some drinks. "But it was never meant to be more than a part-time gig until I could get my career back on track. But I couldn't abandon my girls or clients when business took off. My business had grown too big. Too much was at stake."

"Did you have any direct contact with any of the customers?" Jersey inquired.

Without thinking, Beck answered, "Rarely ever. As you can imagine, many of my clients prefer their anonymity. They usually set up their meetings through my office by requesting a meeting with a girl on a certain date. All fees are paid in advance directly to Madam Monroe's Relationship Consulting Service; to avoid any unwanted attention should the police question them. In which case, they would deny any monetary transaction of any kind and would be lovers having an affair. Since no money transactions occur directly between my girls and their clients, that's technically all they are. Clandestine lovers."

"Of your regulars, were any of these high rollers government officials?"

"I'm simply not at liberty to disclose that information, ladies. You know how it is."

Jersey grabbed Beck by her arm and twisted it behind her back. Slapping on a pair of handcuffs, she said, "I'll tell you how it is... I'm arresting you for suspicion of murder regarding Senator Mark Durrell."

Beck's, partially from shock and partially from the pinch of her arm being bent in an unruly manner. "What do you mean you're arresting me for suspicion of murder?"

Julie was equally caught by surprise. "Based on what evidence?"

Jersey replied, "If all our suspects have been eliminated, except for one, then chances are they're the one we're looking for." Process of elimination. It's fairly standard procedure, Kingston. You should look into it sometime." Without another word, Jersey escorted Kateland Rameses Beckensale away.

"Procedure my ass," Julie huffed under her breath. Julie knew two things. The first was that Beck wasn't smart enough to assassinate anyone, let alone pull it off in the way the senator and his girls had died. And second, she knew that Beck was dreadfully afraid of snakes. She wouldn't get caught within a mile of one, even if her life depended on it.

The only question that lingered in Julie's mind was, why now? Why, all of a sudden, was Jersey Blair trying to derail the investigation? Was it just a ploy to score brownie points with Washington to gain an advantage over Julie, who was always one-upping her and making her look bad, or did she know something Julie didn't? Julie had a thousand other questions, but her cell phone buzzed before she could consider them.

Pulling out her golden iPhone, Julie saw a text from her partner, John Scarecrow. It read:

Meet me at the usual spot. Foun₁ something you'll be intereste₁ in.

Julie walked back into the mansion, but instead of heading back out the way she'd come, she made a detour past the kitchen, down the adjoining hallway, and followed it to the door that led into the five-car garage.

Upon entering the garage, a large smile appeared on Julie's face. Beck had an Aston Martin Vantage, an Audi R8, and a hot pink Jaguar F-Type. "Well, she's got good taste," Julie said. "That."

It was no big secret that Julie had a thing for cars. Probably because her father had been a grease monkey, he'd fix up his hot rods in his spare time when he wasn't busy fixing other people's cars. He was a gearhead, and his enthusiasm for cars must have worn off on her because, as far back as she could remember, she'd always loved cars. The smell of an oily garage, the sound of engines revving, and the chatter of the mechanics all brought back fond memories of her father from her childhood.

Cars were the only thing still connecting her to the memories of her father—she had been too young when he died to remember much else. Which is why, standing in Beck's garage, Julie couldn't help but feel a sense of nostalgia. Moreover, she felt a strong temptation.

Julie had always wanted to drive an Aston Martin. It was the car of choice for all super agents, from James Bond to Johnny English. A large grin crossed Julie's face when she opened the key rack on the wall next to the door. She found all the keys for every vehicle neatly on display.

"I'm sure she won't mind me borrowing it to come save her sorry ass," Julie said aloud as if finding a valid reason would make grand theft morally justifiable.

Outside, the housekeeper returned to the poolside with a pitcher of lemonade and a tray of glasses, but nobody was there.

She glanced around, wondering where they could have gone, when the rumble of a V12 engine roared in the distance. She shrugged and figured they had gone out for lunch.

As the car drove off and vanished, the housekeeper put the lemonade down on the patio table. Plopping down into the lawn chair, she snatched up the Vanity Fair magazines on the glass coffee table beside her and thumbed to the featured article. It was a showcase piece about the epic return of a favorite starlet, Kateland Rameses Beckensale.

The housekeeper, whose name was Carla Rodriguez, although nobody ever cared to learn it, rolled her eyes, took a sip of lemonade, and muttered in Spanish the same advice she had been giving Beckensale for years.

"Si quieres atrapar peces, primero ebe conseguir su culo mojao."

In rough translation, it meant, "If you want to catch a fish, you must first get your hands wet."

Although she always made it a habit to share this sagely wisdom with her employer, Beck never seemed to understand. She was trying to say, "If you want something badly enough, you first have to pay the price."

Well, at least she could feel comforted knowing that she had given the eviction today, even if it was only to the visage of Beck staring back at her from the magazine's pages.

Feeling drowsy, the housekeeper put her feet up, lay back in the chair, and covered her face with the magazine, beginning her afternoon catnap.

15

Stool Pigeon

LEANING BACK IN HIS CHAIR, BLAKE "THE RAZOR" McDoogle watched his guest approach the glass window of the visitor's booth and take a seat. Picking up the phone, he waited for his caller to do the same, then asked, "To what do I owe the pleasure of your visit, Detective?"

John Scarecrow looked long and hard at the felon, studying the natural signs of aging in the man's weathered face, the salt-and-pepper tufts on the sides, and the deep wrinkles of crow's feet that formed when Blake smiled at him. "I've come to ask you a couple of questions."

Slicking back his primarily black hair, McDoogle leaned back in his chair again and thought momentarily. "In that case, I grant you two questions about what kindness remains of my withered old heart."

"Will you answer honestly?" Scarecrow inquired.

Raising his right hand, McDoogle replied, "God as my witness. But you see, Detective, you now have only one question left."

"Did you coerce your wife to try to take out Julie Kingston?"

Leaning forward again, McDoogle flashed Scarecrow another big, toothy grin. "What? Did something happen, Detective? You know, being on the inside, then it's a sweet time."

"You know very well what I mean."

"Assuming I did, and assuming I could manage such a feat, as you can see, I'm pretty much trapped here like a damned orange and black clownfish," McDoogle complained as he tugged on his standard issue, bright orange prison inmate uniform. "But it seems you're fishing for a motive."

"It's nothing personal," Scarecrow reminded him. "But it's my job to investigate all possible suspects."

"You'd think," McDoogle said, rubbing the stubble on his chin, "that being locked up in a federal prison would be a pretty air-tight alibi."

"That doesn't answer my question. Did you or didn't you order the hit?"

"Honestly?"

"Honestly," Scarecrow replied.

"Nobody double-crosses me. Nobody takes my livelihood and fortune and gets away with it. Nobody dishonors me, and if they do, you can be sure they'll sleep with one eye open at night. I didn't get the nickname "The Razor" for nothing, you know?"

"So what you're saying then is you have anger management issues?"

Blake laughed and sat back in his chair. He eyed John Scarecrow with an amused sort of grin. "You're not intimidated by me in the least, are you?"

"Not really," Scarecrow answered.

"Most people would be cowering in my presence. Sure, they'd try to mask it with a brave face, but they'd still reek of fear. The look in their eyes always betrays them. But you... I'm having trouble getting a read on you. That unholy mask you wear is probably throwing me off."

Touching his face, Scarecrow looked puzzled for a moment. "Mask? This isn't a..."

"But to answer your question," McDoogle interrupted, not giving Scarecrow the chance to enlighten the criminal, "Kingston is the one who put me behind bars," he said, rubbing his finger through his oily hair once again. "So, of course, I get a hard-on anytime her name gets mentioned." As for the ex, "Mrs. Razor," she took everything I had and then some. So I figured, why not kill two birds with one stone? Better yet, why not have the first bird kill the second bird and then ruin herself in the process?"

"So you admit to manipulating her, then?"

"Beck is Play-Doh in my hands," McDoogle said, making sculpting motions with both hands. "But who's to say what was going through Beck's head? Certainly not I. Besides, unless you have some tangible evidence against me, it sounds like this is more of an unfounded accusation than a substantiated one. Keep fishing, Detective. Perhaps someday you'll become skilled at it.

Staring back at the prisoner, Scarecrow smiled once and then just as quickly grew serious again. "Does the name Tiffany Blair mean anything to you?"

"That'd be three questions now, wouldn't it?" McDoogle said with a curt smile.

"Technically, you didn't answer my second question. All you did was duck it."

As the priest sang, the guard informed them that their time was up. McDoogle smiled once more, briefly, then said, "I enjoyed our little chat. Really. It was lovely to hear that my two favorite ladies are doing well."

McDoogle hung up the phone, waved goodbye, and waited for the guard to usher him back to his prison cell.

Scarecrow couldn't help but feel overly protective of both Julie and Beck because they were his two favorite ladies. And he'd do anything to ensure their safety and well-being.

HAVING RETURNED TO HIS PRISON CELL, MCDOOGLE LAY down on his cot and started whistling "This Old Man Came Rolling Home." Suddenly, an annoying buzz interrupted him, and his cell door slid open. Sitting up, he saw two guards take their position outside the door, and then John Scarecrow strode in.

"What's he doing here?" McDoogle demanded to know as he stood up, wagging his finger at Scarecrow. The guards squared their shoulders, silently replying with an ironic reply.

"You know I'm friends with the warden, right?" Scarecrow said, pointing at McDoogle, then himself.

"I don't care if you're friends with Jesus H. Christ, you don't just get to barge in here like you own the place."

"I don't think you realize how this works," Scarecrow relayed. "You don't have rights. You relinquished your rights when you broke the law. When you killed all those people. So when I ask you a question, I expect an answer."

"Well," McDoogle chuckled, "you've got a big pair on you if you think for one second that you can barge in here and make me turn tricks for you like some show dog."

"No, I don't expect you to do anything for me other than serve out your life sentence."

"So if you already know you're just wasting your breath with me, then why bother me?"

"Do you know what an *ahnentafel* is?"

"An *ahnfel*...what?"

"It's another name for a family genealogy that's written in a way that doesn't require a family tree. Counties keep them in the registry to help track registered voters, past and present. Your name is stricken from the catalogue if you are incarcerated, but the record remains. Everyone you're related to is right there in that little book."

"So why are you telling me this?"

"You see, I did some research and found out that you have a sister."

"A half-sister," McDoogle corrected. "And how did you find out about that? Nobody knows about that except for my sister and me."

"You're right. Under normal circumstances, your names wouldn't appear together unless your parents had additional siblings.

McDoogle eyed the Scarecrow and then gave up, backing down. "Go ahead, Detective. I have the feeling you're going to tell me anyway."

"After your father remarried, he and his second wife had a child, but they ensured the child would be born on a belated honeymoon in Mexico, so as not to have a record of the birth in the United States. Getting back across the border was easy since a newborn doesn't need a passport as long as both parents show they are legal citizens."

"So, what of it?" McDoogle pried.

"You're forgetting that we live in the twenty-first century, the age of the genome. I had to get a court order to retrieve your genetic profile from your trial. Lo and behold, your DNA matches a young girl born in Mexico but never acquired U.S. citizenship. Your sister Tiffany. Additionally, and just as fascinating, it seems you both share a half-sister with your mother but a different father. A half-sister named Jersey Blair. But I assume you already knew all this?"

McDoogle sat still, staring at Scarecrow in silence. His lack of words spoke volumes.

"It's interesting the types of people we find we're related to. "It makes tracing one's genealogy truly exciting, don't you think?" Scarecrow asked, a demure smile forming on his burlap face.

McDoogle folded his arms and frowned, obviously displeased by the conversation's turn. He didn't like people prying into his personal affairs. "What are you implying, then?"

"I'm not implying anything, sir. But if you knew that your half-sister Jersey was carrying out a vendetta against those she perceived to be your kin's killer, I'm sure I could find enough incentive to compel you to share such a valuable piece of information with me."

"What kind of incentive?" McDoogle asked, raising an eyebrow.

"Well, seeing as how you're serving three back-to-back life sentences, cutting time off your sentence is out of the question. But getting you a better cell, a fluffier pillow perhaps, that sort of thing."

McDoogle had to stop himself from laughing out loud. "There you go making assumptions again, Detective. You assume I'll help you because I have no reason not to. Right? But here's a little secret. I hate cops. I hate people in general. That's why I'm here. I love to hate. And I love killing more. So, as you can see, unless you bring me something more significant than a family tree, I'm afraid I'm out of luck."

"I'm offering you the carrot here," Scarecrow informed. "Don't make me take it back."

"Are you threatening me?" McDoogle stood up and got in Scarecrow's face. He stared at him with the cold gaze of a killer.

John Scarecrow suddenly broke the tension by rubbing his temples and saying in a deep, resonant voice, "I'm generally courageous, but I seem to have a headache today."

While McDoogle continued to eyeball Scarecrow, he stealthily slipped a shank out from his sleeve. It was a toothbrush with two razor blades wedged on either side of the head, all held tight with rubber bands.

"I'll answer one last question if you answer one of mine," McDoogle said as a crooked grin crawled across his otherwise stone-cold face. "tit-for-tat, if you will."

"Deal," Scarecrow replied.

"Do I make you nervous?"

"Not especially."

"Does it bother you more that I killed twelve people on the outside or that I skinned them alive?"

"You're asking me to choose between two evils, where there is no lesser evil in the eyes of the law. Killing and torture are both wrong."

"That's the consensus, anyway," McDoogle laughed. Then, with lightning-quick reflexes, McDoogle swiped the blade, aiming to cut Scarecrow's jugular. But just as he made his move, the lights flickered, going out for a brief moment, causing him to lose sight of his target, then just as suddenly they came back on again.

McDoogle held the shank in his hand and looked around the room. He couldn't believe his eyes. The whole bloody cell was empty. Stranger still, it was all locked up tight. The door was sealed shut, and the two guards posted outside were nowhere to be found. There was not a trace of anyone, least of all the Scarecrow. It was as if they had never been there at all. McDoogle ran his hand through his greasy hair and tried to wrap his mind around it.

"Funny," McDoogle said to himself. "He left without answering his burning question. "Looking down at this bed, McDoogle saw a strange object resting on his pillow. It was a neatly folded origami crane. Walking over it, picking it up, holding it to the light, and inspecting it. Making out a trace of writing on the inside fold, he unfolded the paper, flattened it on his bed, and then read the message.

My last question is this: Has the ghost of your sordid past returned to haunt us all?

"That's for me to know and you to find out," McDoogle answered with a sneer. He then tore up the letter and threw it on the floor.

16

Suspicions of Foul Play

MUNCHING ON A BLUEBERRY BAGEL CAKE WITH CREAM cheese, Julie leaned back in the diner chair, looked at John from across the table, and flashed him a pithy grin. "What is it?" she asked. "Why are you looking at me like that?"

"Like what?" John asked, taking off his fedora. John set it on the table and brushed the wispy strands of doll-like hair from his face.

"I don't know... Likely, you can't decide whether to ask me out on a date or tell me my grandmother died."

"Oh, by the way, how is your nan doing?"

"She's doing well. Had her hip replaced in October of this past year. She said she needed it to stop the wobble that was affecting her aim at the shooting range. I told her it wasn't the hip so much as the caliber that was throwing her off. I recommended she trade down and try something other than the .45, but she wasn't having any of it."

"You got to love your nanna," Scarecrow chirped.

"Yeah," Julie said, thinking fondly of her. But I'm fairly certain you didn't take me out for bagels to discuss Nana's health.

"Well, as much as I care about your nana, you'd be right. You're not going to believe this," Scarecrow informed, "but Jersey Blair has a notorious stepbrother, and he's none other than our old pal Blake 'The Razor' McDoogle."

A silent calm came over Julie as she fell deep into thought. Her chewing slowed, and right when she was about to stop to swallow, she took another bite. "So you're thinking the hit on me, the threats against Beck, and the murder of these prostitutes might all be connected somehow?"

"Honestly, I'm not sure what to think. But something is bugging me about this string of events."

"I know exactly what you mean. There doesn't seem to be any clear motive behind any of them."

"Apart from Blake's attempt at revenge."

"Yeah, apart from that."

"Buteventhatstrikesmeasodd.Asifitweremeantasadistractio nforsomethingbigger."

"Bigger? Like what?"

"Well, we all know his disdain for you and his ex, but was the risk worth it? I mean, having a cop killed and framing Beck for it wouldn't have just made the headlines, it would be damning when the lead back to him. It would have likely landed Blake on death row. So..."

"So…" Julie cut in. "You're thinking maybe he had no choice in the matter?"

"Right."

"But the only person who could get to him would likely be Jersey Blair herself."

"The question is," Scarecrow said as he rubbed his chin, "what does she have on Black that would get him so scared that he'd be willing to risk a certain death sentence?"

"Assuming he had succeeded, we wouldn't be on this case regarding the mysterious string of homicides related to Senator Durrell. So, the other question is, who would know that would be working on the case in my absence?

"Jersey Blair," Scarecrow answered.

"Right. And if Beckensale were out of the way, it would be the final nail in the coffin of her call girl service, which would be put permanently out of commission."

Suddenly, Scarecrow snapped his fingers and looked at Julie with big eyes and an impossibly wide grin. "What if, and this is just a theory, but what if the senator was the intended target from the beginning?

Julie raised an eyebrow. "Goon."

"Okay," Scarecrow said, panning his hands like a movie director. "It's like this. The FBI has something on the senator. Assume they find some skeletons rattling around in the senator's closet."

"Like the death of a prostitute?"

"More like the death of several," Scarecrow said, pinning his pointer finger to the table to emphasize his point. "What if our strangled victim wasn't the first?"

"I certainly hope you have something for me, because you're barely getting by."

Scarecrow pulled an envelope from his breast pocket and slid it across the table to Julie. He looked at her face as she opened it and looked at him in shock.

"You've got to be kidding me."

"It's all right there," Scarecrow said.

"It's fracking longer than my laundry and grocery lists combined."

"So you see my point now? The government becomes aware of these overseas expenditures and initiates an investigation. What they find is a trail of women's bodies following the senator's globetrotting from Thailand to Singapore, from South Korea to the Philippines."

"All Asian countries," Julie said with wretched revelation, her stomach beginning to churn.

"Your hunch that the senator's racism was deep-seated seems accurate. What we couldn't have foreseen is the fact that he was a serial killer of women."

"So the government finds out about these incidents and then, like any civilized government, tries to sweep it all under the rug."

"Naturally. Something of this magnitude could never be made public. It would stir up an international crisis. The minority populations would be outraged. All the countries of the victims would be outraged. Everyone would be demanding retribution. So what better way to eliminate the problem than to play his vices against him? Make it look like an accident."

"So you're saying Tiffany Blair was a plant?"

"I don't have anything substantial, but it certainly fits. She's a veritable ghost. After the hit, all she'd have to do is disappear across the border and retire in sunny Mexico. Nobody would have been the wiser."

"Apart from your theory, we still haven't pinned down anything concrete."

"Right," Scarecrow acknowledged. "My hunch is that Jersey Blair couldn't find anything on Senator Durelle either, so she took matters into her own hands. It's not a far stretch of the imagination. After all, she had family ties to organized crime. What if Tiffany Blair got recruited by big sis to assassinate the senator?

"What if all went according to plan and the unforeseen change in venues gave the Blair sisters the window of opportunity to explain why the senator's regulars couldn't be of service? After that, the rest is easy. The plan was put into place, and the evening proceeded as usual. Once alone with the senator, our assassin began strangling him. After all, the senator was accustomed to that sort of thing. However, things suddenly took a turn for the worse on that fateful night.

"The senator must have realized that his life was in danger, a violent struggle ensued, and the senator, in a fight for his life, got the upper hand and proceeded to strangle his strangler."

"Ironic twist of events, if true," Julie asserted, still chewing on her blueberry bagel. "But then what about our other girls? What about *Snow White and the Seven Whores?* They were all poisoned."

John smiled. "Seven women dead, except for the final call girl, who mysteriously vanished."

"Right," Julie answered.

John kept smiling.

"Why do I feel you know something I don't?"

"Because," John said in a pleased tone, "I think I may have just figured out who your mysterious fourth woman is."

Julie shot him a surprised look. "Really? Who?"

"Jersey Blair."

"Dammit," Julie cursed, pounding her open palm with a clenched fist. "Why didn't I see that? She must have been the other woman. It makes total sense, assuming she's carrying out a vendetta to avenge the death of her sister. A murder which could never be mentioned due to the sensitive nature of it all."

"Now we're talking," Scarecrow said, pointing at Julie's eyes and drawing an imaginary line to his. "But then, on the night of the murder, our vigilante of justice shows up only to find the senator with two off the street hookers, which puts a kink in her whole operation. So she slips in the bad batch of cocaine, originally intended for the senator, and gets rid of any potential eyewitnesses."

"Right, but you're forgetting the crushed larynx," Julie reminded, drawing a slit across her throat with her thumbnail.

"It was an act of revenge. Of course, our killer wanted the senator to know who she was. She wanted to see the fear in his eyes as he squeezed down until she could gasp no more."

"But then poor Snow White comes along and stumbles upon a triple homicide in progress. Snow White becomes collateral damage, but no Prince Charming can rescue her this time."

"Meanwhile, all we've been doing this whole time is chasing our shadows." Scarecrow rubbed his chin briefly, then said, "I have only one theory, but I'm afraid it's not a very good one."

"I'll take a bad theory over nothing," Julie said, brushing her bangs away from her eyes.

"Maybe it's true what they say; the bad apple doesn't fall far from the tree."

"Are you saying Tiffany Blair was a psychotic killer like her brother?"

It would explain why Jersey initially enlisted her. Blake "The Razor" is behind bars, so you go to the next best thing. Little sis gets skilled, and you devote the rest of your life to trying to take down a snake, ironically enough, by poisoning people with the snake's venom. However, as I mentioned, it's just a flawed theory. More of a hunch."

"Okay," Julie said, stuffing the last morsel of bagel in her mouth, "you get on this and see if you can connect Jersey to the crime scene. Determine where the poison was obtained and how. We need something solid; otherwise, we'll never nail this down."

"I'm already on it," John said as he picked up his fedora.

"I'm going to call in some favors south of the border and see what kind of dirt I can dig up on this Tiffany Blair chick."

John turned to head toward his brown-to-red Honda Fit hybrid car when Julie called out to him.

"Wait a minute..."

John turned around.

"You didn't do the paper, cranking thing, did you?"

"How did you know?"

"Because you haven't talked about how it went with McDoogle. Usually, you'd be spilling your beans, every detail, unless you didn't want me to know something. You did some of your magic voodoo mumbo-jumbo that I explicitly ordered you not to do."

"The Magician's Swan Song is a perfect, well-respected illusion!" Scarecrow said defensively.

"Accept that it's not an illusion when you do it!" Julie fired back.

"But he tried to cut me with a razor!" Scarecrow added in his defense.

"No excuses," Julie said. "You know what happens when you use actual magic."

"Natural disasters abound," Scarecrow grumbled as he looked up at the sky with a frown.

"Right. Somewhere in the world, either in the next few hours or even in the next couple of days, an earthquake, flood, or tsunami will occur, putting thousands of lives in jeopardy.

Or an iceberg will break off and float harmlessly out into the Pacific, where it'll melt. No harm, no foul."

Julie shot him the evil eye. "No more magic. Consider it an order."

Scarecrow sighed and turned back toward his car. "Yes, boss. No more magic."

"Oh, and thanks for the bagels!" Julie said just as Scarecrow was climbing into his car. Not hearing her, he drove off. Across the street stood a man wearing a Burning Man, full of braids and beads woven right into it, staring at Julie in panic-stricken terror. In his hands was an alien conspiracy sign with a large green bobble-head E.T. painted on it, reading, "The End is Nigh!" They Walk Among Us."

Julie instantly devised a hundred and one ways to mess with him, but she decided the most subtle approach would be best. Raising her forehead to her lips, she hushed him with a long, drawn-out sigh. "Shhh," and then climbed nonchalantly into her borrowed Aston Martin Vantage.

She revved the V12 engine and slammed down on the gas, the tires squealing as they attempted to gain purchase on the cool asphalt. Rubber smoking, the Vantage raced off at a breakneck pace, leaving him standing there to suffer whatever conspiracy-theory panic attack his delusional mind had inflicted upon him.

17

¿Qué Nos Trae La Serpiente?

RECESS WAS LET OUT, AND SO SOON ENOUGH, THE schoolyard was abuzz with the squeals of children running and laughing, their sugar highs at fifty screams per minute. Across the street from the schoolyards, a nervous-looking Mexican American in his early fifties.

Plopping down in the seat next to him was a stunning athletic woman wearing a sleeveless, grey, dry-fit running top with sweat stains from her afternoon jog. Her form-hugging jogging tight was flashy purple, and tucked inside her ears were some Beats earbuds.

Dabbing herself off with a towel, the woman looked at him and said, "Good, I'm glad you got my message."

"It's almost as if that joke never gets sold for you. Look," he said, pointing at the primary school across the street, then at himself, "It's July down by the schoolyard."

"Public places are still the safest place for those who want to blend in and not stick out."

"Not for people in protective custody, I can assure you. Public places make men nervous. More chances of someone recognizing me."

"Really? Do you think one of those children playing over there might recognize you?"

Julio eyed the children suspiciously, then sighed a long, drawn-out sigh. "I guess not." Turning toward the woman, he inquired, "So, Detective Kingston, to what do I owe the pleasure of this visit?"

"It's Lieutenant now."

"Moving up in the world, I see."

"How's Camila and the kids?"

They're doing as well as expected, especially considering they must use fake names whenever they go to school or the grocery store. But we'll manage. God willing, we'll manage."

Julie sat back on the bench and watched the children play in silence.

"Have you ever thought you'd have kids?" Julio asked.

"God no!" Julio gasped, taken totally off guard. "Hell to the capital no." Shooting Julio a wide-eyed look of exasperation, she asked, "Don't you know me at all?"

Julio chuckled and turned his head as the chime sounded and children swarmed into the school. It was like watching a reverse flood. "Seeing as I'm not getting any younger, how can I help you, Lieutenant?"

Julie skipped any further pleasantries and got straight to business. "When you were working as a double agent with the

DEA to infiltrate Juan Diego's drug cartel, you once told me a story about a snake-woman. I'm curious about the specific details of that story."

Julio raised his eyebrow, which looked like a caterpillar trying to climb over his sweaty forehead, and grumbled, "Why in the world do you want to hear that old superstitious bit of folklore?"

"I have my reasons," Julie replied. Putting her hand on his, she whispered, "Please."

"Well, I'm not the most remarkable storyteller, but it goes like this. They say that one day, out of the blue, a Chica Blanca appeared in the small town of Reynosa. Nobody knows where she came from or who she was, but they thought she was just a child. As the legend has it, she was no more than fifteen or sixteen, and having been abandoned and made destitute, it wasn't long before a typical pimp came upon her and brutally assaulted her. They beat and ravaged her to within an inch of her life, the dogs. But the girl's will to live was strong, and she crawled to a nearby shack.

What she didn't know was that it was a secret, out-of-the-way safe house for Juan Diego, who was keeping a low profile after hearing that the DEA had infiltrated local chapters of the cartel. Taking pity on the poor girl, he took her in and raised her as his own until she was grown.

"I've heard all this before. I know that Diego raised her, trained her to be a deadly assassin, and then let her loose on those who would defy his authority."

"You don't know that Diego taught the girl self-restraint and discipline. He made her more than just deadly. He made her cold. On her twenty-first birthday, Diego held a seaside beach party. The whole town, including the young men who had raped her all those years ago, showed up for the big event. That night, she seduced the young men, lay with them, and even though it must have been her worst nightmare come true, their nightmare was beginning. For them. It is said she paralyzed them with the venom of a viper, and as they lay dying, she sawed off their manhood with a piece of broken glass, then skinned them alive and bathed in their blood."

"Sounds like my kind of woman," Julie quipped.

Julio's eyebrow rose so high that Julie was sure it would leap off his face.

"We don't joke about the *Serpiente Femenina*."

"I'm beginning to get that," Julie replied seriously. "What about the rest of the legend? What about the massacre?"

"Yes, the massacre. As you probably know, our little girl had grown to love killing. That night on the beach, she exacted her revenge and paid back in full, but still, it could not fill the dark emptiness within her. Gradually, the townsfolk grew weary of her, and soon they banded together, forming a mob, and marched to the shack that Diego had given her. They called her out, but she refused. So they burned the shack to the ground. Inside was the charred husk of a young woman."

"This is where it gets interesting," Julie said, her eyes wide, as she waited to hear the rest.

However, over the next month, people began disappearing from the village. Nobody knew where they were disappearing to or whether they had been kidnapped or met with some unfortunate accident. Day by day, people vanished—women, children, and even people's dogs.

Eventually, the state police were called in, but by the time they arrived, nothing was left but a ghost town. A day later, the police dogs happened upon a mass burial ground, which contained the remains of everyone from the village. Every living thing had been inexplicably poisoned with a snake's venom. Some say it was the *Serpiente Femenina*, and others believeitwasherghostthatgotrevengethatnightforthosewhobur nedheraliveas well as those who stood by and did nothing to stop it."

"But that's not true, is it?"

"Nobody knows what is true and what isn't anymore. That's why they call it a legend."

"I heard rumors, rumors that there was another story."

"Sí, there is a much stranger story."

I haven't heard this one yet. Please go on."

"At about the time of the massacre, your own country had the case of the mysterious snake-man. I believe you were the one who caught him, no?"

"I was," Julie confirmed. "A man by the name of Petros Dillahunty confessed to attacking campers, hikers, and outdoor mountain bikers. As you may know, venom."

"Down south, the story is a little different. People say that it was the *Serpiente Femenina*."

"Impossible. Petros confessed."

"A confession can be bought, Lieutenant. Especially when you are knee-deep in the corrupt world of drug lords and their unlimited wealth and power."

"Is there more to the story than that?"

"Not much. But there is a stranger story that you may be interested in."

Julie couldn't imagine a story stranger than the last, but her curiosity was piqued. Leaning in, she nodded to let Julio know she was very interested.

Julio said, "One of your hotshot American supercops, an FBI agent working alongside the DEA, busted Juan Diego about five years ago, around the same time as your Snake-Man incident. Now, Diego's luck had run out, and he got fatally wounded in the crossfire.

When the agents finally found him, he was already dead. But in his pocket, they found a piece of paper with jotted coordinates. Believing it to be the warehouse where Diego kept this product, they raided it only to find a massive, empty storage facility. But in the basement of that facility, there was a room."

"What kind of room?" Julie asked with bated breath.

"A room with dark secrets. Plastered on the walls of the small room were photographs of dozens of skinned victims cut out from newspaper clippings of a sinister man's killing spree. A man named..."

"Blake 'The Razor' McDoogle."

"You know of him?"

"I'm the one who put him behind bars," Julie said, her mind still spinning as she tried to piece these events together.

"Well, then, Lieutenant Kingston, I feel I should warn you. One photo stood out among the rest."

"Stood out how?"

"It was the only one that didn't belong."

"How so?"

"It was a picture of a woman. She wasn't any ordinary woman either. She was an officer."

"Whose picture was it?"

"Remember the FBI woman who had tracked down Diego?"

"Yes."

"Thepicturewasbutamererereflectionstaringbackather.Itwastheagentherself."

"Does this woman have a name?"

"If I recall correctly, she had a rather famous-sounding name. Something like Jersey Shore."

"Do you by any chance mean Jersey Blair?"

"Yes, that was it. Jersey Blair."

"I knew it," Julie said, pounding her palm with her fist.

"You see, Lieutenant, the FBI agent had come the closest anyone ever has to catching the *Serpiente Femenina*. But instead, all she found was herself amid a collection of death and chaos. That is how the *Serpiente Femenina* works.

"Some say he is the hellspawn of Satan's unholy union with an earthwoman. Some say he is a pure manifestation of evil. Whatever he is, there is one thing I am certain of..."

"What's that?" Julie inquired before Julio had a chance to finish.

"She is still out there. The *Serpiente Femenina* still walks among us—disguised as one of us—and she strikes when we least expect it, like the viper from which she steals her venom. By the time you realize who she is, it's already too late."

"Thanks for the stories," Julie mumbled, still chewing on the information and trying to piece together something more plausible than urban legends.

With that, Julius slowly got up, shrugged, and said reassuringly, "That's all they are, just stories." Then he walked off without saying another word.

Julie remained in her seat, staring blankly at the side of the road, trying to separate fact from fiction. Whatever the truth was, she was afraid that whatever the hell was going on, these strange events were taking her down a dark and dangerous path. Once she had set upon it, there would be no turning back.

18

Protective Custody

KATELAND RAMESES BECKENSALE DEMANDED SHE BE TAKEN to the safehouse before she answered any further questions. With her long, elegant legs stretched out and her feet on the table, Beckleanedbackinherchairandmadesuretoarchherbackjustenou ghtocausetheswellofherbreaststobulgeoutofthetopofhertank- topsothatDetectiverookieJackWolfe, who stood in the corner of the interrogation room, could better admire the rise and fall of her feminine form.

Jersey looked at Julie and shrugged as if to say it was a reasonable request.

"Fine," Julie stated, having no choice but to concede to the conditions. "But I'm going with you," she insisted, brushing her hair out of her eyes.

Satisfied with the answer, Jersey signaled Jack with a nod, and they left the room. Julie put her palms down onto the interrogation table, leaned forward, and looked deep into Beck's dark brown eyes.

"Ju, again, I can't thank you enough for not pressing charges," Beck said sincerely.

"I just don't know why you didn't tell me sooner that Black was threatening you. Beck, I know I can be rough around the edges, hot-tempered, and obtuse sometimes, but if you're ever in trouble, don't hesitate to call me."

Beck leaned forward so that her nose was practically touching Julie's. As she stared back into Julie's emerald eyes, Beck sighed. "I guess I just didn't have my head screwed straight. With the new movie having just wrapped up, I haven't had time to settle into my mind, it seems."

"Well, I'm going to keep you safe now," Julie said, shooting Beck a warm smile.

Beck put her hand on Julie's, and the warmth of her touch sent a charge through both women. "If there is any way I can make it up to you," she said, flashing a playful smile," just let me know."

"Anything?"

"Anything at all," Beck said in her sultry southern accent.

Julie smiled back deviously. "There is something. But I may be asking a bit much of you."

"I doubt it," Beck said, her breathing growing heavy. "I would put myself out there for you. I'd open myself up for you. I'd let you have your way with me if you wanted."

"As much as I appreciate that, Beck, I sort of had something else on mind."

Herlip shoving just mere centimeters away from Julie's, Beckensale huffed dreamily, "Well, girl can fantasize, can't she?"

Julie smiled endearingly back at Beck. She didn't know what was happening between them, but was more attracted to Beck. Julie wasn't even going to begin to try to quantify her feelings. After all, in her mind, there was no gay or straight controversy. She felt it came down to just one thing: people loving people. Plain and simple. She didn't know why that wasn't good enough for me. It was damn well good enough for her.

Although she didn't mind Beck's constant flirting so much, she found it distracting. It confused things, and she needed to keep a clear head and focus on the case. She pulled away and let the spark fade before it could turn into a flame, then she explained to Beck precisely what she needed him to do.

BECK FOUND AGENT JACK WOLFE DRINKING A COFFEE IN the cafeteria. She made her way to his table and sat down next to him. He smiled at her, but was unexpectedly caught up in the intensity of her smoldering brown eyes. Also, the fact that she was like Angelina Jolie and Scarlett Johansson all rolled up into one mega-babe was something he liked about her—what he wanted even better was that she was currently single.

"What can I do for you?" Jack asked, his voice nearly cracking due to his light-headed excitement. Jack cleared his throat to ensure his excitement wasn't mistaken for boyish charm.

"It depends," Beck said, the corners of her mouth curling up into a sensual smile. "I've been feeling a little, I don't know, insecure lately. I guess it's because of everything that's going on in my life. The past few weeks have been a little dizzying to say the least." Beck leaned in, wrapped her arms around his, feigning a bit of vertigo, and batted her eyelashes at him. "I guess I need a shoulder to lean on most. If that's all right with you?"

Jack Wolf smiled. "Of course. No problem. After all, a policeman's job isn't just about catching bad guys. We also must serve and protect the public," he said.

"Well then," Beck sighed. "I have one idea how you may be able to serve me." Leaning in, she whispered the details into his ear.

Jack nearly fainted when he heard what she had in mind. Tugging on his collar, he turned to Beck and smiled. "Yes, ma'am," he answered. "You'll be glad to know I've got protection in my back pocket, and I can serve you any way you please. I mean, if that's really what you want?"

"Enough talking," Beck said with authority. Grabbing his hand, she eagerly pulled him out of his seat and guided him toward the restroom at the back. Before passing through the door, they were making out like a couple of hot and bothered teenagers.

Stumbling into the bathroom, Beck swiftly peeled off her tank top. Her breasts suddenly bounced back down into their proper place, revealing the sexy black brassiere she wore underneath. Leaning in for another kiss, she suddenly shoved Jack backward, and he fell into the bathroom stall.

The metal door flapped at the two clambering into the stall. Beck kissed Jack's mouth and fumbled trying to unbutton his shirt at the same time. After struggling with the buttons, she became frustrated and tore his shirt off, half of the buttons popping off as she pulled it down over his shoulders. Jack didn't care, though, while being seduced by Hollywood's leading lady.

Beck peeled his shirt the rest of the way down around his shoulders, making it hard for him to move his arms, like a straitjacket, but he didn't think anything of it. Bending over, she rubbed her hands up and down his thighs, then unfastened his belt. Jack's pants slipped to his ankles, and he fumbled a bit to keep his balance. With his arms and legs immobilized, he felt a bit like a caterpillar awkwardly trying to squirm his way into position. Rising backup, Beck abruptly shoved Jack down onto the toilet. Unable to catch his balance, he nearly fell into the open bowl.

Beck grinned at the shocked look as he landed on the seat with a thud. "I hope you like it rough," she said, licking her lips seductively.

"Actually," Jack informed, "I've had a rough day. Would you mind playing nice?"

"I hate to break it to you, big boy, but all is fair in love and sex. What's the matter? Am I too much of a woman for you?"

"No, it's not that. It's just…"

Before Jack could finish his sentence, Beck leaned in and nuzzled his earlobe, giving him a light bite with her teeth. The sensation of her hot, moist breath on his neck sent shivers down his spine and caused him to forget what he was going to say.

Beck had him right where he wanted him. Stopping short of his lips, Beck smiled mischievously as if she wouldn't continue. Before Jack could realize that it wasn't at ease, all he heard was the clank of handcuffs that she had slipped out of his back pocket and onto his wrists. Looking down, Jack discovered his wrists shackled to the piping of the toilet. Beck pulled back, leaving him high and dry, and grabbed her tank top and put it back on.

"Um, look, I'd usually be up for this sort of thing, but... do you mind unhooking me?"

"That depends," Beck said.

"Depending on what?"

"On whether or not it would be okay."

Perplexed, Detective Jack Wolfe asked in a shrill voice," Why wouldn't it be okay?"

That's when they heard the sound of the toilet flush in the neighboring stall.

Jack gulped." Somebody else is in here," he said in a hushed tone.

"I know," Beck replied in her usual voice, no longer putting on an act of seduction. The stall doors swung open, and Jack's face suddenly became austere. Julie Kingston stood before them, casually eyeing the scene.

Julie leaned in and put her arm around Beck, who playfully nudged Julie's ear with her nose. The two women looked down at poor, manipulated Jack.

"Next time you get in bed with the Feds, make sure you don't f@#k up the case by spilling sensitive information while the blonde is humping your brains out."

"I've been played, haven't I?" Jack asked with a voice full of disappointment.

"Like a fiddle," Julie said with a vengeful grin.

"What gave me away?"

"Your perpetual hard-on for every skirt, except for Jersey, for starters. That could only mean one thing: You were already tapping that hot piece of ass." Julie paused, waiting for him to deny the accusation, but he diverted his eyes—a guilty gesture if there ever was one.

Julie said," More noticeably, when Jersey got back first, I put two and two together. Unless the FBI is into the habit of tapping police headquarters, someone must have tipped her off. Then there was the fact that Blake was spooked long before we had a chance to question him. Something had him so rattled that this lips were sealed tighter than a fresh jailbait's asshole in the prison showers.

"At first, I couldn't figure out what had spooked him so badly, but it could only have been a message from Jersey. The prodigal's return had majorly upset him, but according to visitor records, she hadn't been in to see him. So, I checked the prison visitor log for on-duty officers, and lo and behold, you had been in to see him a full day prior. What did she have you say to him that made him scared shitless?"

Jack let out a defeated sigh." Honestly, I don't know. The message didn't make all that much sense."

Beck paused long enough to stop molesting Julie's ass and chimed in. "What do you mean it didn't make sense?"

"Her message wasn't about anything in particular. It was strange."

Both women looked at him, eagerly waiting to hear the message. 'Well?" Julie said impatiently. "Spill it."

"The message was simply, 'Remember Mexico.' Like I said, it doesn't make any sense."

"Actually," Julie said, ruffling Jack's perfectly molded hair to annoy him," it makes perfect sense." With that, the restroom.

Beck reached down and grabbed Jack by the scruff of his neck, pulled him in one last time, and gave him a deep, sultry kiss.

"Word of advice," Beck said, still holding tight to Jack's hair, "Office romances never last." Then, following Julie's lead, she winked at Jack and left the way she had come.

"Wait! It was a rookie mistake. I won't make it again. Promise! You can't just leave me here," Jack pleaded, but they were already gone. Pausing for a bit, Jack called out, "Hello? Anyone there? Anyone at all?"

Butallhereceivedwasthereplyofhisownvoiceechoingofftheb athroomwalls. Slamming his head into the side of the stall, Jack muttered to himself, "Balls."

19

Faceoff With the Devil

PULLING UP BEHIND THE BLUE CARRERA GT, THE SILVER Aston Martin stopped in the driveway of the safe house high in the Hollywood Hills. The mansion was a modern design featuring an unconventional, block-like architecture that stood out among the older mansions on the drive. It primarily consisted of thirty-five-foot glass panel walls framed by eco-friendly woodwork with sharp ninety-degree corners. It had a great view of the city high upon the hill.

Julie's idea was to hide. Beck, a Hollywood actress, lived amid the upscale lifestyles of the rich and famous. In other words, plant the needle in a stack of needles. Blending in was the best way to disappear. Beck was sure to be safe.

Jersey had brought Beck ahead of time because Julie had to swing downtown to pick up John Scarecrow. Although she could have asked him to meet them there, she thought personally bringing him up to speed would be better.

John looked excitedly over at Julie as they sat in the car. "I'm telling you, it was a bona fide ninja sighting!"

"I think you've been watching too many kung-fu movies again."

"Kung-fu is related to classic Chinese martial arts, whereas ninjas and samurai are from Japan," John informed her grandly, correcting her in the politest way possible. After all, he knew his partner had a short fuse and didn't want to set her off.

"I didn't mean to offend," Julie laughed.

"No offense taken." John winked at his partner, then got out of the car. "Still, do you think it's wise to leave Beck inside with a suspected killer?"

"You really are smitten with her, aren't you? "Julie inquired.

"Beck? Well, yeah. Kind of." Scarecrow said, scratching the back of his head. He was almost embarrassed to admit it, but Julie knew him well enough for him not to need to hide it. He couldn't sneak anything past her.

"Don't worry about Beck. If Jersey is trying to get revenge for her sister's death, she'll try to make it look like an accident. Poisoning Beck now would be a clear giveaway that she was the killer, so she'll bide her time."

"It seems like a big gamble," John replied.

"Beck has been briefed on everything. She knows what she's getting into."

Getting out of the car and shutting the door, Julie looked over at John, who was approaching her side. "I think I might best start warming up to her myself."

"You totally meant for each other," John said reassuringly.

"It's just that..." Julie stopped mid-sentence.

"Just what?"

"This whole falling in love with a girl thing. I know I shouldn't care about that, but I just... It's new. It's a little bit scary, if you know what I mean. What if she doesn't feel the same way back?"

As they approached the mansion's door together, John reassured her, "Hey, don't worry about that. Beck is totally into you. When she's around you, she can barely contain herself."

"It's that obvious, is it?"

"Yeah, pretty much." John stopped at the top step and looked at Julie. "Hold up, wasn't Special Agent Jack Wolfe supposed to meet us here?"

Sticking with telling the God's honest truth, Julie informed," Actually, he won't be able to make it after all. He got tied up with something else."

"Oh, I see," John said.

"I can't tell you're broken up about it," Julie laughed.

"Hey, who am I to complain? I get to spend time trapped in an undisclosed mansion with gorgeous women overlooking the city lights at night."

Julie reached down to grab the door handle. "Ever the romantic, you are."

Johnwatchedcuriouslyas Julie'sfacewentfromanamusedsmil etoastonecoldlook.

"What's the matter?" asked John.

She raised the palm of her hand and showed it to John. Moist red stains glistened on her palm like stigmata.

"Is that blood?" John asked, squinting under the soft glow of the porchlight.

Pushing open the door discreetly, Julie drew her sidearm and put her finger to her lip, letting John know she was going silent. With catlike steps, she cautiously entered the home.

Checking the various chokepoints, Julie cautiously aimed her gun at every entrance. John followed closely behind and provided cover.

Making their way into the living room, Julie heard a soft thud from behind the sofa. She motioned to John to go around the other side.

As they closed the chair, Julie saw black pants. She quickly came around to find Jersey Blair clutching her right arm. A large gash cut into her flesh, and it was bleeding profusely.

"Don't worry about me," groaned Jersey, trying to fend off the sharp pain. "You've got to rescue Beckensale. He took her out back."

"He?" Scarecrow asked.

"The killer," Jersey informed. "I went to the bathroom for just a moment, and when I came out, he was already on top of her, trying to force the poison down her throat. I managed to pry him off of her, but then he pulled a blade on me and…"

"Is he still on the premises?" Julie interrupted, scanning the room.

"That's what I'm trying to say," Jersey replied, taking a big gulp, trying not to let the pain cause her voice to rise. "He stepped out the back door the moment you arrived."

Julie motioned with the barrel of her gun for John to take care of Jersey. "Stay here," she demanded. "I'm going after him."

Bending down, John tore the tattered sleeve from Jersey's arm and made it into a tourniquet, tying off her wound.

Stepping stealthily up to the glass patio doors, Julie edged along the wall toward the entrance leading out to the back pool.

Once she got close enough to peer out of the glass, trying to be as quiet as possible, she slid the door open and stepped out onto the back patio. The glow of the pool lights and the rippling water created a blue illumination that danced around everything it touched.

At the end of the pool, Julie saw a dark figure holding Beck hostage. It was a male with a hood, a long Bowie knife pressed to Beck's throat.

"Julie!" Beck cried out.

"Who are you? "Julie demanded, aiming.

"What do you mean, who am I? I'm your friend, Beck!"

Julie sighed. She would have done a face-palm, but maintaining her aim prevented her from expressing the actual depth of her frustration. "Not you," Julie informed, motioning toward Beck's. "*Him.*"

"Put down the weapon, or your girlfriend dies," boomed a deep, rattling voice. Masked by the mechanical sounds, it was clear that the man had a mask on.

"What do you want?"

The man began to slice into Beck's shirt and slowly cut it open, revealing her voluptuous bust wrapped tightly in a sexy, burgundy brassiere. Slowly, he dragged his blade across her breasts, slicing them very lightly.

"*Aieeeee!*" Becks screamed out.

Julie fired a shot at the villain's head.

BLAM!

The shot hit this forehead, dead-center, but ricocheted off, grazing Beck's shoulder. She screamed again.

Unable to advance, Juliet took drastic measures and fired a shot through Beck's right leg. Beck screamed even louder, "*AIEEEE!*"

The bullet passed through and hit the assassin in his leg. The bullet penetrated his thigh and caused him to stumble back briefly. Luckily, this strategy let Beck break free just long enough to give Julie a clear shot.

Before Julie could fire off another round, however, the assassin quickly spun around, and with his menacing blade, he sliced the back of Beck's legs and kicked her into the pool.

Without his human shield to protect him, Julie opened fire. Blasting away didn't seem to work since the man's body armor merely absorbed the impact of the bullets as if they were nothing more than pellets from an air gun. Julie aimed at his head and fired her last shot.

With lightning reflexes, the assassin deflected the bullet with his knife. With a sharp clang, the bullet ricocheted, but this time, it shattered his blade. The severed blade fell to the ground with a clatter.

Just then, the man hit the panel on the side of his neck, his mask opened with a hiss of compressed air.

Julie beheld two creepy, yellow-eyed sunglasses with tinted lenses. They were snake's eyes.

"I was not expecting that," Julie muttered to herself.

Beck flailed her arms miserably, trying to pull herself to the surface of the water, but she'd been immobilized by the slash to the back of her legs, and the bullet wound to her shoulder made it impossible to swim correctly. Sinking to the bottom, her lungs burning to get a gasp of air, she let out a flurry of bubbles and was swallowed by the water. Her eyes widened with fear as she slowly drowned.

Julie yanked out the empty clip and popped in another as she aggressively charged forward. Running along the pool's edge, she fired rapidly until her secondary clip was spent. Julie released that clip and slid in her backup one, now only a few meters away from the villain.

The snake-man smiled, showing his fangs, and leaped off the edge of the elevated patio and disappeared into the thicket of the trees that ran to the bottom of the hill. Julie ranted to the edge and looked over, the shuffling of trees and a mixed-up tangle of shadows.

"Shit!" Julie cursed. Tossing her gun away in frustration, she immediately turned back around and dove into the pool.

Reaching around Beck's arms, Juli kicked hard, and the two women rose to the surface.

John arrived with Jersey Blair just as Julie surfaced with Beck, and they helped pull both women out of the pool. Listening for Beck's heartbeat, panic-filled Julie. "Her heart has stopped!"

Full of adrenaline, Julie crawled up to Beck and began administering CPR. Pinching her nose, Julie put her mouth to Beck's chest and pumped Beck's chest three times, blew into her mouth again, and repeated.

"It's not working!" John said in a distraught voice.

"The suspect is getting away," Jersey said, drawing her sidearm. With one arm, limping, she turned to the group and said, "I'll get him. "With that, she took off after the killer.

"Wait!" John called out.

"It's fine," Julie said. "You go back there for her." Not wasting any more time, Julie climbed onto Beck's torso with both hands." Don't die on me, you crazy-ass bitch!"

Scarecrow dashed into the thicket of trees and headed down the hill in hot pursuit of the killer and Special Agent Blair.

20

Bombshell Threat in Blonde

BECK SPEWED WATER OUT, GAGGED, AND COUGHED, THEN took a throat-rattling gulp of fresh air.

Julie grabbed Beck's face and kissed her squarely on the lips in a moment of pure, exuberant relief. "You had me worried out of my mind," Julie bawled, tears streaming out of the corners of her eyes.

Beck sat up and embraced Julie, and the two women hugged each other and cried.

"Why did you shoot me?" Beck sobbed into Julie's warm embrace.

Julie pulled her in tightly. "Sorry about that. I didn't have any choice. It was the only way to save you."

Beck's sobbing suddenly changed to small laughs. Through a clutter of shivering teeth, she said, "I just realized, you shooting me makes use even for the other week. I'm sorry I shot you."

"I'm sorry I shot you, too!" Julie lamented.

Laughing together, Juliet took Beck's hand and clasped it tightly. Looking into each other's eyes, the veil of all pretenses was lifted away, and all that remained were their bare souls. Julie leaned in and kissed Beck again, her lips pressing gently into Beck's, but her hesitation melted away this time.

As a surge of ecstatic energy shot between them, what began as one of the most delicate kisses in the history of kisses turned into tongues and lips biting. As passion overcame them, Beck pulled Julie down onto her and kissed her back with the same unbridled passion.

SCARECROW SHOT THROUGH THE GROVE OF TREES AND stepped out onto the asphalt. Looking around, he spotted Jersey up the road. She was standing next to the suspect, and for a moment, he thought they were talking to one another. Once Special Agent Blair noticed him, however, she put the gun to the villain's head.

"Wait!" John shouted, extending his hand, but it was too late. She had already pulled the trigger.

Scarecrow ran up to the body and checked his pulse, but he was dead. Looking up at Jersey, he frowned. "Why did you go and do a thing like that?"

"It was necessary. In my condition, I wouldn't have been able to fend him off."

"But I could have provided backup."

"I didn't know you were coming," Jersey lied. "Besides, in such situations, you can only react."

Scarecrow stood up and paced back and forth for a minute. Their one lead into the mysterious assassinations had dried up, and it no longer seemed that Jersey was a suspect, although she was undoubtedly acting suspicious.

As she nervously paced, Jersey bent down again, reached into the killer's jacket, and pulled out a cigarette lighter. She lit herself a cigarette and then looked back up at Scarecrow, who stared at her in shock.

"What?" Jersey mumbled, the cigarette teetering on the edge of her lip." You have a problem with me smoking?"

"Besides the fact that smoking will kill you?"

"Yeah," Jersey laughed, taking another drag on the cigarette.

"Well, besides tampering with a crime scene, which is its own can of worms and a ton of paperwork, it's just that…"

"Just what?" she asked, shooting him an impatient look.

"How did you know the lighter was in his pocket?"

"Lucky guess," Jersey answered. "Lots of people keep lighters in their jackets."

"But you knew exactly which pocket. You didn't frisk or search him and went straight for the lighter. That could only mean one thing. You knew him personally, and you knew where the lighter was there because he's lit your cigarette before." He shot her a stern look, adding, "Bad habits and all that."

Jersey puffed on the cigarette, then looked down at the lighter in her hand. "Well, shit," she said, realizing her foolish mistake.

"Was he working for you, and you killed him before he could give you away? That way, Jersey Blair lives to kill another day?"

"Something like that," Jersey answered, flicking her cigarette to the ground and stomping it out with her boot heel. "I guess congratulations are in order, Detective."

"Why are you not more worried, Special Agent Blair?"

"Because, if you must know, Special Agent Blair is dead. She has been for a very long time."

Scarecrow's eyes widened with revelation. "Tiffany? Tiffany Blair?"

"I'm surprised you didn't figure it out sooner. You'd come the closest of anyone."

"All I needed was a little more time," Scarecrow assured her. "I would have figured it out eventually. If not me, then Lieutenant Kingston."

"So, what hung you up, Detective?" Tiffany Blair asked, flicking the light on, then clamping the lids shut, only to repeat the process. The clacking of stainless steel sounded ominous.

"I just couldn't figure out why Jersey Blair was so hell-bent on getting revenge for a sister she hardly even knew. None of it made any sense. But as it turns out, it was the other way around. You were getting revenge on the man who killed your big sister."

"It wasn't just about the revenge. It was about the opportunity. You see, Jersey came to me all those years ago and wanted me to go undercover for her, but I wasn't comfortable with it. It seemed too much like a setup. When I refused, she shed herself and went in my place. When Senator Durrell killed her, I knew things would have gone differently if I had just helped my sister like she had asked.

"I made it my vendetta to get payback no matter the cost. I became a call girl, worked my way up the organization, and eventually became one of the senator's regulars. Prim and proper Special Agent Blair by day, profligate, seasoned whore by night. I threw myself into each role and became those women. I fooled drug lords, I fooled the FBI, and I fooled you, too. And I would have kept fooling everyone if I hadn't given in to the smallest of vices—a stupid cigarette."

"But why poison all those innocent women? Why leaves so much death and carnage in your wake?"

Tiffany clapped the lid of the lighter shut and looked up at Scarecrow with cold, penetrating eyes. "The FBI was too cowardly to bring the senator's transgressions into light and promptly restricted the information. So, I decided to do what I do best. Leave a trail of death and carnage so great that they couldn't be ignored."

"So unable to use his actual murders to incriminate him, you hoped to frame the senator for a whole batch of different murders, is that it?"

"Oh, he was guilty of his fair share, alright, but I didn't want to let him get away squeaky clean when he was the dirtiest worm that ever lived. I wanted that son of a bitch to rot—prison or open fields somewhere. It didn't matter to me how, just as long as he paid for his crimes and his lifeless carcass was meat for the vultures. My plan would have worked, too, but then I got careless."

"Snow White?"

"She was a regrettable mistake," Tiffany said, disingenuously.

"No, that's not it," Scarecrow said, circling Blair, who watched him from the corner of her eye." You intended for her to die like all the rest. That's why you set up your brother, Blake 'The Razor' McDoogle, to fall for you. But why? Trying to fill your brother's notorious shoes, perhaps?"

"My brother is a fool. All he cares about is power. But killing is an art. And like any art, masterpieces cannot be rushed." Tiffany said, biting her tongue, not even attempting to conceal that she enjoyed the pain. Composing herself, she smiled again.

"Blake is a true psychopath. Naturally, there is the suffering of others. I didn't even have to twist his arm. He was more than happy to take Lieutenant Kingston and that Hollywood whore out for me. As for Snow White, I couldn't help myself. She was beautiful and innocent-looking. She didn't belong in this world of darkness and corruption. As far as anyone should be concerned, I did her a favor."

Tiffany turned, faced Scarecrow, and smiled at him with an unnervingly manic grin.

Reaching into his jacket pocket, Scarecrow retrieved a set of handcuffs. Extending them toward Tiffany, he said, "If you don't mind?"

"Oh, but you see…" Tiffany began. Bending back down, she fetched a small black tin can from inside the dead man's jacket and then turned back to face Scarecrow." I do mind."

Suddenly, Tiffany squirted Scarecrow with lighter fluid. Jumping back in fright, Scarecrow cried out, "What's this?"

Lighting the cigarette lighter with a crisp flick of the wheel flint, Tiffany smiled and then tossed it. Scarecrow watched the lighter's spirit through the air as if in slow motion, then the flame licked his sleeve. Almost instantaneously, his jacket sleeve was set ablaze, and before he knew it, his entire arm had giant orange flames growing from it.

A vicious grin curled onto Tiffany Blair's face, and she could hardly stop herself from laughing as she watched the flames consume the Scarecrow. As she burned, she remarked, "It looks like you were right after all, Detective. Cigarettes do kill."

"No!" a voice cried out, and Julie emerged from the nearby tree line and dashed to where Scarecrow was flailing, orange flames crawling onto his back.

Peeling off her wet leather jacket, Julie used it to try to put out the flames. Wrestling Scarecrow to the ground, she finally got him put out, but not much of his limbs remained. Both of his arms were completely burned away, and his face was half charred. Even his legs were singed. Worst of all, he was barely alive.

"I'm afraid," he wheezed, and taking a deep breath he said, "'Twas brillig, and the slithy toves, Did gyre and gimble in the wabe, All mimsy were the borogroves, And the momerathes outgrabe."

With his last line coming to a close, Scarecrow's eye sockets went dark, and the white, marble-like eyes that showed such spirit faded completely away.

"Don't die on me!" Julie screamed down at him. That's when she felt the muzzle of a gun pressed to the top of her head.

"And here I thought you'd be the one to catch me finally."

Julie looked up at the woman holding the gun to her head with the unnerving blend of an angry scowl and a giddy grin. As Julie's mind raced to figure out what was happening. All the puzzle pieces fell into place, and finally, it dawned on her.

"Goddammit!" she cursed, kicking herself for her foolishness. "I've been Keyser Soze'd!"

"The greatest trick the Devil ever pulled was convincing the world that it didn't exist," Blair gloated, giving an even more sinister smile.

"You threw me off by feigning ignorance about the snake's venom. You know about it all too well. I should have figured as much. After all, nobody is that stupid. At least not anyone who strived to be an FBI agent."

Tiffany Blair shrugged as if to say, "So what?" and then pressed the muzzle of the gun even harder into Julie's forehead.

"Now what?" Julie asked, looking up past the gun barrel at the captor.

"Now, you die, I'm afraid."

Julie smiled curtly and then let out a terse chuckle. This unexpected reaction threw Tiffany Blair off her game and, luckily, distracted her from her murderous task.

"What's so funny?"

"Honestly," Julie said, leaning into the gun, showing that she wasn't afraid, "I expected more from the notorious *Serpiente Femenina.*"

"Sorry to disappoint," Tiffany remarked. "But when you're as good as I am, the killing is easy. Sometimes you forget what a real challenge feels like. But I must admit, Lieutenant, you and your partner proved to be the best challenges since I dismantled Juan Diego's drug empire."

"What do you mean, you dismantled Diego's drug empire? I thought the one who saved you back in Mexico?"

"He saved me from the streets, but he made me his sex slave. Do you know how many abortions he forced me to have?"

"I'm sorry you had to endure that hardship," Julie said.

"I was fifteen!" Tiffany roared, rage flooding her veins and causing her to tremble.

Taking a deep breath, she centered herself and found the willpower to continue her harrowing tale. "After getting my revenge on that godforsaken town, I went into hiding. I picked out a new name, an alias, and began to live a new life free from my past. That's when Jersey tracked me down and offered me a once-in-a-lifetime deal. But I didn't want to get involved in the assassination of an American politician, as I'd have the CIA, FBI, NSA, and anyone else with a badge hunting me for the rest of my life."

Tiffany took a deep breath and then continued. "A few weeks after turning down the offer, I heard of my sister's death, so I took her identity and faked my death, and I set out after Diego myself, swearing on my sister's honor that I'd hunt him to the ends of the Earth if I had to. And there was no place he could run. No place he could hide. After all, he taught me to think exactly like him. Taking him down made Jersey Blair a legend within the FBI and I was a free woman. From then on, I could write my ticket."

"Now, will you just kill me, already?" Julie complained, sharing her best fake smile.

"What? Why?" Tiffany asked.

"Because your incessant monologuing is too agonizing to bear."

Both women stare at each other with a mutual disdain so powerful it could have ignited sparks between them.

Tiffany shrugged again and, squeezing down on the triggers slightly, said, "Well, if you insist."

BANG! THE GUNSHOT ECHOED UP AND DOWN THE DIMLY lit road, only a streetlight at the top of the bend providing any light. Julie fell onto her back, her face frozen in wide-eyed fear. Looking up at the stars, Julie thought everything would fade to black, but then, nothing happened. Sitting up abruptly, Julie checked herself for bullet wounds. Again, nothing.

Astonished that she wasn't dead, Julie looked around until she saw Jersey Blair, or Tiffany Blair, or whoever the hell she was, with a bullet hole through the side of her head, lying right next to her. Blood pooled around her head, while the snake-man in the body armor lay just a few feet beyond her, and to her other side lay a still-smoldering scarecrow.

"You alright, Lieutenant?" a man's voice called out.

Looking around, Julie saw Detective Jack Wolfe jogging toward her, holding his gun by his side.

Looking down at the body of Tiffany Blair, then the backup at Jack, Julie said in perplexed exasperation, "Dude, you killed the girl you were porking."

"As it turns out," Jack replied," she was madder than a hatter."

"True enough," Julie muttered, shaking her head in disbelief.

Things had not turned out as she'd expected, but that was life.

Extending his hand, Jack helped Julie up. Keeping her grip, Julie squeezed hard, letting him know how thankful she was. "Thanks. And I'm not just saying that as your boss. I owe you one."

"No problem," Jack said. "Just doing my job. Also, the paramedics are back at the house, attending to Ms. Beckensale. Just thought you'd like to know that."

"Thanks," Julie said, giving him a grateful nod. "Just out of curiosity though, how on God's green earth did you get out of those handcuffs so fast?"

"Cleaning lady found me. Soon rather than later, thank goodness. After some screaming, she alerted everyone, and Captain Greenblatte rescued me from the porcelain prison. He wasn't at all thrilled about it, though. You'll probably get an earful when you return to the precinct."

"Thanks for the heads up," Julie answered.

"Holy crap!" Jack blurted out upon seeing the charred remains of Scarecrow lying despondent on the ground. "What happened to him?"

"Fire," Julie answered.

"Will he be alright?"

"Most likely," Julie replied. "He quoted Lewis Carroll."

"Doesn't he always do that?"

"Well, yeah. But I'd like to think he would think of other things if he were really about to check out."

"Should I call an ambulance, or…something?" Jack was at a loss for words. It wasn't every day that he had to save an actual living, breathing scarecrow from the brink of death.

Drying a tear from her eyes as she looked down at Scarecrow's burned husk, Julie answered, "Don't worry about him. I'll take him to see a good witch doctor. I know who can fix him so he'll be right as rain." Nodding at Tiffany Blair and the mysterious snake-man's lifeless bodies, she added, "You deal with this mess."

"Right," Jack answered, putting both hands on his hips. He didn't know what was stranger, the fact that two dead bodies and a barely pulsing pile of straw littered the street before him, or the fact that his boss was making house calls to an honest-to-God witch doctor.

Julie Kingston smiled on the last time, her thoughts drifting back to Beck. Turning around, she headed back up the road toward the mansion. She departed, waved over her shoulder, and addressed Detective Wolfe without looking back. "You did good, rook. There may be hope for you yet."

TEST SCREENING

Galactic Time-Traveling Cowgirl Super-Cop Cleopatra

SHOOTING SCRIPT

21

Attack Of the Killer Mutant Cephalopod

"Darling!" Johnny said, gripping the buxom brunette Roxy Ricochet by her waist and pulling her in tight. "I love you! I've always loved you. That's why I'm asking you, Roxy, please, stay here in the past with me. Don't go back... to the future."

They stood atop the Empire State Building with an armada of Nazi Zeppelins dotting the sky behind them. Just then, the observation tower doors blasted open, and two Nazi soldiers ran onto the promenade. Ignoring the Nazi threat, Roxy looked into Savior's eyes and said, "Excuse me a moment."

Reaching down, she slid up her royal purple cocktail dress and pulled out the Walther P.P.K. tucked inside her garter.

Just as quickly as the Nazi foot soldiers raised their weapons and aimed at their targets, Roxy locked lips with Savior, and without so much as looking, held her gun out and fired. The Nazi scum dropped where they stood and crashed to the ground before they could ever get off a clean shot.

"You were always a natural," Savior said, complementing the buxom heroine.

Roxy handed Savior her gun and said, "Here, take this. Something to remember me by. Besides, you're better than I am."

Savior took the gun and cocked it. At that exact moment, one of the Zeppelins exploded overhead as a Godzilla-sized octopus clinging to the side of the Empire State Building, waltzed out of the sky with one of its gargantuan tentacles. The other blimps loitering about aimed their machine guns at the massive monstrosity and began spitting hot needles of white fire into it, pelting the beast with a furious barrage of bullets.

Walking to the ledge, Savior tucked the gun into his flight jacket and stripped off the jetpack from one of the dead Nazi foot soldiers and strapped it on. Looking back on one last time at Roxy, he shot her his trademark debonair grin, a wink, and said, "Here's looking at you, kid."

Roxyblewhimadapperkissandwatchedas Saviorpulleddown hisflightgoggles, smashed down onto the control button he held in his right hand, and flew off into the surrounding fire and chaos. "Be careful," she called out after him.

Not one to be left out of a firefight, Roxy Ricochet walked over to a large black cello case, bent down, and opened it. Economically tucked inside the case was a massive Gatling gun with a stabilizer and a whole chain belt of ammunition. Pulling it out, Roxy Ricochet threaded the bullets into the loading mechanism. Holding the massive gun by her hip with her dress flapping in the wind, Roxy Ricochet opened fire on the other Zeppelin that hovered in the sky.

"WHAT THE HELL IS THIS MOVIE EVEN ABOUT?" JULIE Kingston interrupted.

"Hush now," Beck reprimanded, shoulder.

Sitting a couple of seats down from them was Captain Greenblatte. "Why do I have to be here?" he asked in unconcealed annoyance.

"Because we all value and respect your opinion, sir," Julie says sarcastically.

"Don't blow smoke up my ass," the captain grumbled.

"Oh, my favorite part is coming up," Beck said giddily, giving Julie's arm an affectionate squeeze.

Julie gave Becka a peck on the lips, and the two women snuggled up together, getting even cozier than they already had been.

Just then, stumbling up the aisle, came Jack Wolfe. "Sorry," he whispered, stepping gingerly up the aisle and trying not to step on any toes. "Had to stand in line forever to get these Milk Duds."

"Zip it," a gruff voice growled. "I can't hear the bloody movie with all this jibber-jabber." Jack took his seat next to Doctor Baudrillard and apologized. "Sorry, Doc."

"I don't get it," Greenblatte said aloud. "If Roxy Ricochet is the main lead, why is Cleopatra the film's title?"

Jack turned to look up at Captain Greenblatte, who sat directly behind them. "Roxy Ricochet is Cleopatra from the future! In the first movie, a mad scientist returned and kidnapped Cleopatra and imprisoned her in the future."

"*Ohhh,*" Greenblatt said, in revelation. "What's the first film called?"

"Time Traveling Queen Cleopatra vs. the Alien Invasion," Jack informed him, his words garbled as he stuffed Milk Duds into his face.

Beck leaned over and whispered toward Greenblatte, "It's a trilogy."

"Good to know," Greenblatt intoned, holding his hand to accept some complimentary Milk Duds from Jack.

"For Pete's sake! Can you people be any noisier?" a familiar voice griped.

Julie turned in her seat and smiled at an old friend. "Sorry, Scary. We'll try and keep it down. Just so you know," Julie said, her face beaming with joy, "I'm glad to have your back."

"It's good to be back. This new straw packing is top notch," Scarecrow said, flexing his new, slightly bigger arm and patting his bicep.

It looked as if Julie was about to say something more, but Scarecrow put a gloved finger to his lips to let her know quiet time had resumed.

Upon the screen, the monstrous cephalopod climbed atop the mooring tower of the Empire State Building. Roxy Ricochet turned and launched a volley of fire into the massive beast's beak.

The Gatling gun glowed red hot as its white-hot needles at the monstrosity. However, the bullets only aggravated the Octo-Terror even more than it already was. With one mighty swipe of one of its gargantuan tentacles, it sent Roxy flying over the edge of the building.

Screaming, she was sure she would become a human pancake batter on the pavement. Just then, Johnny Savior swooped down in his rocket-powered jetpack and snatched Roxy up into his arms.

"I got you," he said, smiling big and bright.

As they flew up into the sky again, they broke through the canopy of clouds and saw a glorious sun rising, stretching out as far as the eye could see across an ocean of white mist. Never was there a more perfect moment for a more perfect kiss.

"So, have you given it any thought?" Savior asked. "I mean, about staying with me here in New York?"

"I have," Roxy answered, running her finger through his hair. "And there's something I have to tell you, Johnny."

Savior smiled even more, giving him an artificial manic appearance, as he answered, "Yes, anything, my love."

"It's just that," Roxy said, touching his chest. "I don't love you."

"What?" Savior laughed, unable to believe his ears.

Remembering the gun she had given him earlier, she slipped her hand inside his jacket, to where he'd stashed it before catching her, and drew it out. Placing its muzzle under his masculine jaw, she flashed him her pearly white smile and kissed him goodbye. Savior's eyes widened with dread, but Roxy pulled the trigger before he could even react.

BLAM!

Free-falling, Roxy unfastened the rocket-propelled jet pack and peeled Savior's corpse out of it. Falling at terminal velocity, she hastened to fasten the straps around herself. Without time to spare, she pulled the strap securing herself to the ignition button. The jet pack lit up like a torch, and its rockets squealed at full throttle, fighting against the force of gravity.

Slowing to a halt, Roxy set down on Liberty Island, belching smoke from the jet pack's exhaust. As she stripped off the spent jet pack, a Nazi SS officer in an elegant black uniform with an armband sporting the swastika approached her. Standing mere feet away, he stared at Roxy with a disdainful look and asked, "Is it done?"

Roxy pulled out a small tube from between her breasts, popped it open, and added some red lipstick to her full lips. "The flyboy is out of commission. He'll no longer be a thorn in our side."

The Nazi officer smiled and said, "Good."

Looking up at him, Roxy asked, "Did you fulfill your part of the bargain? Did you bring me what I asked for?"

"I am a man of my word, Fräulein," the SS officer replied, reaching into his side pocket. Raising up a giant green emerald the size of a tennis ball, he examined it and said, "It seems a trifle thing, this rock. Hardly worth the life of a man. Especially a man like Johnny Savior."

Walking over to him with her characteristic seductive swagger, Roxy hastily grabbed the gem from his hand and smiled. "Savior was no hero. He was a war criminal doing the dirty work of his imperialist masters. Nazi foot soldier or American stormtrooper, in the end, you're all the same old threat to freedom."

"You have a frank way of stating things, Fräulein." With that, the SS officers snapped their fingers, and an entire squad of Nazi soldiers came out of the surroundings and locked down the perimeter. "Which is why I can't let you live."

"What's the meaning of this?" Roxy demanded.

"Let's just say," the SS officer informed her, "I'm taking out a little insurance policy. Framing you for the death of America's favorite hero was just the first step. Making it look like you are a Nazi spy is, how do you Americans say it, the icing on the cake?"

Two soldiers grabbed Roxy by her arms and began to drag her away. What they weren't ready for was her acrobatic talents. Flipping upwards and backward, Roxy landed behind her captors. She slid one of the soldier's pistols out and dispatched his friend by planting a bullet in the base of his skull. Using another as a human shield, she took out the surrounding members. The SS officer made a quick getaway, ducking behind his fellow soldiers for protection as Roxy wasted no time picking them off one by one.

Out of bullets, Roxy tossed the pistol and ran up to the nearest soldier and, grabbing the barrel of his rifle with one hand, clocked him in the jaw with a firmly up-thrust palm. Knocked out cold, the Nazi crashed to the ground and lay sprawled out at her feet. That's when she heard the deep rattling of a throat being cleared.

Turning around, Roxylookeduptoseeaseven-foot-tallbehemothdressedinatight-fittingNaziuniform. She swallowed a nervous gulp and whispered, "You're a big fella, ain't you?"

With that, she let loose a furious barrage of tight-fisted punches, each planting squarely in the large man's gut. But her blows were merely absorbed effortlessly by his incredible mass. Looking back up at the behemoth's undaunted smiling face, Roxy exclaimed, "Well, shit."

Backhanding her, the Nazi giants smacked Roxy across her jaw and sent her freewheeling. She hit the ground with a thud and, groaning, rolled over and spat up blood as the soldier marched up to her and grabbed her by her throat. Choking her with big, meaty hands, he picked her up off her feet and raised her high into the air.

Slowly asphyxiating, Roxy kicked her legs and squirmed, but to no avail. That's when she remembered the giant green emerald she held. Squeezing the emerald tightly in her fist, she raised her arm above her head and brought it crashing onto the giant's head.

Cold-cocked, she dropped her, and both collapsed into a heap on the ground.

The man's drooling mug rested on her ample cleavage. A trail of his blood-stained saliva trickled down between her breasts. "Ew, gross," Roxy hissed as she pushed the man off her body.

Getting onto her feet, Roxy scanned her surroundings for any further signs of danger. Not detecting, she opened her side satchel, dumped the emerald inside, and then stripped off her tattered dress.

Standing on the edge of the base of Liberty Island in nothing but black lingerie, Roxy Ricochet swung the satchel over her shoulder, turned to the screen, winked at the audience, and then dove off the platform and into the dark blue water of New York Harbor.

Panning down onto the dark, navy blue water where Roxy Ricochet had disappeared, the aftermath of ripples slowly dissolved into choppy, blue waves, and the screen faded to black. Just when it seemed the credits would begin to roll, the screen suddenly came back on again.

Underneath the water was the faint glow of yellow and orange lights rising from the deep. Soon, the water began to froth and foam, and breaking through to the surface, they saw the metal form of a giant robot. Embedded inside the glass chest plate was a cockpit, and at the helm of this giant mech-warrior was the busty Roxy Ricochet!

"I've got some calamari fry," she growled, water rushing down from her wet hair and into the crevice of her bulging cleavage, squeezed impossibly tight together by the half-zipped wetsuit she still wore.

The behemoth robot warrior, as massive as the Statue of Liberty, strode onto the docks of Manhattan, shedding water in torrents as it took its first steps onto dry land. Large blades grew from the robot's forearms, followed by spurts of large flames that shot out of the industrial-sized flamethrowers tucked beneath the blades. The robot's back plating opened up, and two giant rocket thrusters emerged. Igniting, the massive robot launched into the sky and approached the beast terrorizing the Empire State Building.

Suddenly, the words "To Be Continued" appeared in bright, bold yellow letters that clanked onto the screen in full Dolby surround sound.

"WHAT DID YOU ALL THINK?" BECK ASKED, LOOKING at the dimly lit faces of her friends.

Munching on a big bucket of buttery popcorn, Scarecrow whispered, "Best. Movie. Ever."

"I rather enjoy it myself," Captain Greenblatt agreed. "It's like an adult version of Doctor Who, but with a female lead and no sidekick."

"Are you kidding me? This entire movie was nonsense! Moreover, it was stupid and contrived!" the doctor complained. "For starters, the main character's name wasn't even Cleopatra. It was Roxy Ricochet. Why put Cleopatra in the title if none of your characters are named that? And don't get me started on the ending. What was that all about?"

Realizing nobody was interested in his film critique, he released a disgruntled sigh, got up, and excused himself from the party. "If you'll pardon me, I'm going to step out for a cigarette break." And with that, the good doctor left the theatre.

"Nobody likes a critic," Julie quipped.

"Best. Movie. Ever," Scarecrow repeated.

As the credits rolled onto the screen, at the sight of the words starring Kateland Rameses Beckensale as Roxy Ricochet, everyone rose to their feet and gave her a standing ovation. Beck blushed and took a slight curtsy as everyone applauded. It was a good end to another trying few weeks. Julie Kingston grabbed Beck by her waist and reeled her in just then.

"Darling!" Julie teased. "I love you. I've always loved…"

BeckhushedJuliewithherindexfingerpressedtohersoftlipsast heonlookersalllaughedtogetheratthecomicalreenactment.

Among close-knit company, Julie and Beck looked deep into each other's eyes and then did the thing which two people madly in love do—they kissed.

THE END

CASEFILE:3

The Case of the Mysterious Phone Call
from the Haunted Hotel California

CLASSIFIED

22

The Haunted Hotel California

Somewhere in the Mojave Desert,
northeast of Barstow, California.

THE ENGINE REVVED, AND THE DARK CHERRY RED '65 Mustang rumbled to a halt on the side of the desert road. It had twin black racing stripes streaking up the hood and a glossy shine, giving the evening moon a run for its money.

Stepping out of the driver's side of the car was an athletic brunette with piercing green eyes. She wore a coal grey tank top and blue denim shorts that hugged every curve. Over the form-fitting tank top, which amplified her chest, she wore a vertical shoulder holster with a police-issued Glock G41 tucked cozily inside.

She shrugged on the neckline of her cut tank to let the warm evening air of the Mojave Desert lap her glowing chest as she looked over at the abandoned and tumbledown hotel standing before her in the middle of absolutely f@#king nowhere.

"Looks vacated. You sure this is the right place?"

The passenger's side door clicked, opened, and a tall, lanky scarecrow stepped out.

The woman didn't seem to mind that an animated strawman was beside her. Truth be told, she was comfortable with him. There was a strong rapport between them, and it seemed they were old souls who had known each other from the dawn of time.

John Scarecrow looked at his partner, Julie Kingston, then back at the derelict roadhouse. Nothing else was around for miles but the desert backdrop and the cerulean-tinted twilight rising high above them.

John straightened his necktie and pulled out his smartphone to double-check the Google Maps location. "The anonymous girl's call came from this location," he informed Julie." Said she'd been kidnapped and was being held against her will in a room with no lights and spooky noises. That's when the call cut out."

Juliejustseemedtoabsorbinhisrecapwithoutsomuchasanod. Butshewascoollikethat.

Looking back at the rundown hotel, he added, "I don't have to say, though, looks kind of Bates-ish, doesn't it?"

"Hopefully, all the psychos stayed home for the evening." Turning toward her partner, she added," And if this turns out to be one of those pranks and I see one of those assholes dressed as a scary-ass clown, I will drop-kick them so hard they'll rethink their entire goddamn existence."

Lieutenant Julie Kingston looked up into the evening sky and watched the bark's purples and blues fade to black, stretching upward into a deep black bath in phosphorescent stars. She had always loved the Mojave night sky. Ever since her dad took her to Calico Ghost Town as a kid, the desert has held a special place in her heart.

Interrupting their idle chitchat was a loud, mechanical clunk. The noise sounded nearby and was immediately followed by the noisy buzz of electricity, which filled the quiet night air with a humming resonance.

Suddenly, the old hotel's sign lit up in neon blue and green, and every single last one of the hotel's lights came on. What had been just a dark, desolate ruin now was lit up with the glow of yellow light and hummed with the crackle of a mysterious energy.

Julie put her hands on her hips and sarcastically quipped, "Nope. That's not freaky at all."

"That's not the half of it," Scarecrow added, pointing over at the downed power lines at the side of the old building.

"You've gotta be friggin' kidding me," Julie grumbled.

Scarecrow started toward the hotel, but stopped when he realized Julie wasn't following him. Turning back around, he asked, "Are you coming?"

"Yeah, sure. I'm letting you get a few spaces before me first. You know, in case any vampire bats fly out."

"Or clowns?"

"God, I hate clowns." Julie whipped out her Glock, popped out the cartridge, and did a quick bullet count. Looking back, she saw Johnny eyeballing her suspiciously. "What? Just in case."

"I never took the superstitious type," Scarecrow said.

Julie found the twinkle in his eye to be a sarcastic one. "I'm not," she confirmed. "But I am the cautious type. And it seems to me we are two steps away from starring in our very own David Lynch movie."

"Well, I'm the curious type," John replied. "Besides, I can't shake the strange feeling that the girl on the other end of the phone was certainly in trouble."

"You do realize that the only reason the San Bernardino County Sheriff's Department is even letting us speak outside our jurisdiction is that they don't want anything to do with the weird paranormal stuff that happens around you when you get in one of your moods."

"It's not a mood. It's an intuition."

"Same difference, if you ask me." Julie let out a sigh and then followed her partner up to the entrance of the dilapidated hotel.

Julie scanned the lobby by peering through the glass windows of the large wooden doors. It looked quaint enough. The inside didn't look half as bad as the weather outside. "It looks clear," she said.

John twisted the brass doorknob and opened the door. It creaked open rather eerily as he poked his head inside and called out, "Hello? Is anybody there?"

There was no reply.

Pushing the door the rest of the way open, the two police detectives stepped inside.

John went straight to the check-in counter and dinged the small bell set out for customers. Leaning on the counter's edge, he waited for a concierge to arrive. After a moment, and with no concierge, he headed it again.

Looking around the lobby, Julie grumbled to herself, muttering obscenities under her breath. She didn't like the vibe this place was giving out.

John looked over the counter to see if there was any ledger with times and dates, anything to give them a clue as to who'd checked in or out of this place, but found diddly-squat. Looking back, who was staring up at the ceiling? "What is it?" he asked.

"Look at that," Julie replied, still gazing upward.

John looked up and beheld the magnificent antique crystal chandelier upon the ceiling. Leisurely strolling up to Julie, he fixed his gaze on the luxurious chandelier. "Ooh, sparkly!" he said in a bedazzled tone. I wonder what an antique like this is doing in a place like this. It has to be expensive."

Julie and Scarecrow both gravitated toward the center of the room, almost as if by some unseen force, and continued admiring the innate ornamental display of crystal-encrusted lights.

Suddenly, Julie felt a shiver shoot up and down her spine. "Did you feel that?"

"Feel what?" asked Scarecrow.

"The room just got colder," she informed. Although it was a balmy 76-degree evening outside, for some odd reason, for some bizarre reason, Julie could now see her breath as she talked. Blowing on her hand, she said, "This is the type of poltergeist-esque nonsense I don't have time to deal with right now."

"Oh, bother," Scarecrow lamented. "We've stepped into a cold spot."

"You mean like those mysterious spaces where the supernatural world and our world collide?"

Grabbing Julie by the shoulders, John scanned the room suspiciously, as if he half expected something to materialize out of the thin air. "Just know, whatever happens next... It's entirely out of my control."

"What do you mean, whatever happens next—"
FZZZWAT!

AN ENERGY BUILDUP SURGED, AND THE BULBS OF the crystal chandelier exploded in chorus. Shimmering violently, the entire chandelier suddenly unhinged and came smashing down around John and Julie.

As Julie ducked down, Scarecrow did his best to shield her from the shards of crystal and glass showering down on them.

Once the commotion was over, everything went dark.

Dusting herself off, Julie complained, "Hell, no. Just...no. I'm not in the mood."

John stood up and straightened his necktie. "All I know is that it takes a majorly powerful source of dark magic to mess with my mojo."

"Great," Julie said, fishing out her flashlight. "Just great."

Clicking on her flashlight, she scanned the hotel. The walls and the interior were not as they had once seemed. Now, everything on the inside was as decrepit as the outside. The wallpaper was cracked and peeling, and rot and ruin were all around. Even the floorboards were rickety and rotting away beneath their feet.

"Well, at least it all matches now," Julie said as she scanned the room with her flashlight.

Soon enough, Scarecrow had his light out too. "It doesn't appear to be more in character."

"Now, please tell me we haven't suddenly crossed over into Silent Hill territory that we're in some *Stranger Things,* Upside-Down, alternate plane of existence type bullshit. Because I don't think my heart could take it."

Scarecrow sensed that Julie's voice weighed heavily with concern, so he didn't take offense at her irritability. "I don't want to cause any alarm, but you might not be too far off with that guess."

Julie turned and looked at her partner. "You'd better be pulling my leg."

"If we fell through a cold spot, we could come out literally anywhere in space and time. The supernatural is quite unpredictable."

Julie just stared at her partner vacantly and blinked. She had no words.

John Scarecrow happily continued explaining things to her about the nature of the supernatural. "Even the cold spots themselves fluctuate, popping in and out of existence, sort of like dark matter, until, after a while, they dry up or reemerge in some other location."

"So, you're telling me, we went into a haunted hotel, fell through a cold spot, and now have popped out in...some... where exactly are we, again?"

"To be honest, I'm not entirely sure." Leaning back, John scratched his ragged chin and looked around. "It seems that my presence here may have caused an overload in the magisterium of the paranormal divide of the nether realm."

"Sorry, Scary, but I don't speak Voodoo," Julie huffed. "Give it to me in plain English."

Waving his hands about, Scarecrow did his best to explain. "Think of it like this... I'm like the positive end of a magnet; that's the good kind of paranormal. Then there's the bad kind of paranormal, like a magnet's negative end. If the positive and negative ends come against each other, they get stuck together. We short-circuited the cold spot in this case by getting stuck and falling through."

"Like Alice passing through the looking glass," Julie said.

"Precisely. My guess is we are..." Scarecrow paused, scratched his head, and looked around. "I'd say we're in an alternate..." Licking his finger, he held it up, as if to test the direction of the airflow, and then said, "Actually, to tell the truth, I have no idea."

"Well, I know exactly how we can find out." Julie ran back toward the entrance where they had first entered the hotel. Scarecrow shrugged and followed her.

Once they stepped underneath the half-moon fanlight of the hotel's entrance and into the fresh night air, Julie let out a horrible shriek.

"What's it?" Scarecrow asked, frantically looking around. His hand was already under his suit jacket, reaching for his piece.

"My baby!" Julie cried out in distress.

She ran up to her car and pressed her hand to the rusty exterior. Its tires had rotted away, and soot and ash covered it. Nothing was left but the discarded shell of what used to be a vibrant, cherry-red muscle car with a polish so perfect it looked sweeter than candy.

Johnstrolleduptohispartnerandputhishandonhershouldera ndtheysharedamomentofsilenceoverthebelovedvehicle.

Spinning around, Julie wagged her finger in John's face. "What the hell, John?! You know my father left that car! I want answers and I want them now!"

"*Gruuugh!*"

Astrangemoanfilledthedesertnightwhichwasmadeextraeeri ebytheashenovercastthatdulledtheskyandmadeeverythingdrear y. Even the moon was but a filtered glow.

Julie shot Scarecrow an icy look.

Throwing up his hands defensively, Scarecrow said, "I'm sorry! I didn't mean for any of this to happen. Honest!"

"*GRUUUUGH!*"

The moan was louder this time, as if whatever made that terrible gut-wrenching sound was getting closer.

Julie and Scarecrow turned to where the noise had come from and noticed a man in a brown business suit shambling toward them at a rather leisurely pace.

His clothes were in tatters, and his skin was rotting off, leaving open patches of muscles and bone. His eyes were white, and he dragged one foot awkwardly as he raised his pallid arms and reached out to them with his crooked, bony fingers. Then he growled, "*Grahhh!*"

"Is that what I think it is? "Julie asked.

"It looks like a zombie," John said excitedly.

Julie shot him the same icy glare as before. "I know it's a zombie, John," she said through clenched teeth. "The question is…why? Why any of it?"

"Watch out!" a voice called out.

Out from the shadows, a young Asian girl wearing a Japanese schoolgirl uniform sprang into view. The moonlight bathed her face and slender legs in its white glow. Although her short plaid skirt could barely conceal her long legs, she felt toward the monster; it didn't bother her.

Drawing out a katana, the girl leaped into the air, and with one swift flash of her blade, she severed the zombie's head clean off.

The creature's head fell to the ground and rolled to Julie's foot, stopping when it hit its toe.

"Cool!" John said, with his usual cheerful glee.

Julie looked down in disgust at the severed head. "Seriously?"

"You two, what are you doing here?" the girl asked. Her voice was calm, but it sounded urgent as if they were an imposition on her.

Julie looked back at the young Asian girl. By the look of her, she couldn't be more than sixteen or seventeen years old.

"We're on our honeymoon, what the hell does it look like we're doing?" Julie snapped.

"I don't actually care what you're doing," the girl answered abruptly. "But whatever it is, you better do it elsewhere. There's a horde of undead headed this way. You won't last the night if you stay here in the open."

"*Ummm*...about that..." Scarecrow interjected, raising a finger.

Disturbed by the prospect of more bad news, Julie sighed again and rolled her eyes. "Now what?"

"We have to stay here for thirty minutes and wait for the cold spot to materialize."

"Suit yourselves," the girls said with calm indifference, and with that, she turned and headed off.

"Wait!" Julie called out. The girl stopped in her tracks and looked back. "I'm coming with you."

"Didn't you hear what I just said?" Scarecrow's voice grew frantic. "We have to stay here, otherwise the cold spot will close permanently, and we'll have no way of returning home!"

"I heard you the first time, and I heard her too, and she said there's a strong force heating monsters heading this way. So, you do what you want. I'm getting the heck out of this sideways ghost town."

Turning back toward the girl, Julien nodded, as if to say "Let's go," and left Scarecrow standing by himself.

Scarecrow raised his hand and beckoned to her one last time. "Wait, Julie! If you stay here longer than an hour, I can't guarantee I'll have enough power to get us home."

Pissed, Julie turned and yelled back, "Well, thenmaybeI'lljustclickmyrubyredstilettostogetherandwishmyse lfbackhome!"

With that, she turned her back on him and went with the Asian girl with the sword and the short skirt.

23

Stranger Happenings

Somewhere in the Mojave Desert,
northeast of Barstow, California.

FEELING LIKE HE HAD LET HIS PARTNER, JULIE KINGSTON, down, John Scarecrow lowered his head and slumped over beside a nearby cactus. Standing alone in the desert, feeling depressed, he tried to figure out how to resolve the series of strange events that had suddenly plagued them.

Suddenly, he heard scuffling sounds and raised his head to see what the commotion was about.

Zombies of all shapes and sizes shuffled by him in all manner of decay. He estimated that about forty or fifty of the infected were strolled by; however, since he wasn't a human, they ignored him and kept to their merry way. For all they knew, he was just a lonesome scarecrow standing in a vast wasteland—

nothing much to marvel at in such apocalyptic times, if you didn't know any better.

Scarecrow sighed and sat down on the desert sand, threw his arms across both knees, and locked his fingers together. Then he planted his forehead on his crossed hands.

Although he hadn't intended to cause this mess, he was determined to do his best to fix it. He'd wait here until Julie came back. He wouldn't leave her behind. Even if the portal closed, he wouldn't abandon his partner. Not to the zombie apocalypse. No way, no how.

"What manner of sad, pathetic creature are you?" a thick, masculine voice asked.

Scarecrow looked up. Standing before him was a gunslinger with a classic Smith & Wesson .44 Magnum aimed at John's head.

Still moping, John lowered his head again, ignoring the potential threat. "I'm not pathetic, just down in the dumps. And if you wouldn't mind terribly, please leave me alone."

Holstering his weapon, the cowboy sat beside Scarecrow and pulled out a pack of cigarettes. "Mind if I smoke?"

Scarecrow sighed. Usually, he was terrified of fire, but right now, he was too depressed to care. "Go ahead."

"Thanks," the cowboy mumbled, the cigarette hanging on his bottom lip. Next, he flipped open his Zippo lighter and tried it a few times, but the flint was worn, and the spark wasn't enough to ignite the wick. All it seemed to want to do was sputter and fizzle out. "Dammit," he groused.

Scarecrowpluckedastrandofloosestrawoutfromthebackofhi sneckandhelditouttothecowboy. "Here, use this."

Taking the piece of straw, the cowboy held it to the lighter, flicked it again, and watched as the sparks leaped onto the dry straw and lit it up. Using the flaming straw, he put it to his cigarette and puffed a few times to get things going. Just as the end of the cigarette grew red hot, he took a long drag and held it. After a moment, he exhaled and said, "Thanks, padre."

"Don't mention it," Scarecrow replied.

After a few moments of silence, the cowboys spoke up. "I'm guessing it's regarding a woman."

"Isn't it always?" said Scarecrow despondently.

"Are you in love with her?"

"She has these crystal-clear green eyes that penetrate your soul. There is so much warmth in them. But when she's angry, they turn dark and hard, like emeralds, but their sparkle never fades."

"Let me guess, she's taken, right?"

"You guess it."

"Is he right for her?"

"If by he you mean she, then yeah. They complement each other perfectly."

"Suppose that leaves you between a rock and a hard place. Not a comfortable situation to be in."

"I suppose. But it's not so bad. Her girlfriend is my other best friend, the universe finds a way to balance things out in the end."

The cowboy stared at Scarecrow long and hard with his steely gaze. His hazel eyes were a lot like Julie's. They'd seen things. They were weathered by experience. "I think you might fall for the wrong sort of women."

Scarecrow blushed. "Oh, you mean... because they're...? No. It's not like that. I mean, they're not...well, you see, it's like this... It's just love. It doesn't matter who or what you are as long as you have real love. That's what matters. I just happened to love them both."

The cowboy turned away, puffed a few times, and shot a smoke ring. Then, with expert timing, he blew a cascade of grey smoke, which pierced the two rings like an arrow piercing a target.

They shared a moment of tranquility as they gazed into the starry night, during which the whole universe seemed to make sense.

"Don't worry, she'll be back," the cowboy said reassuringly.

"I hope so," Scarecrow said.

"By the by, friend," the cowboy added, turning toward Scarecrow. He offered his hand and introduced himself. "I'm Gordon Longstaff."

"John," replied Scarecrow, shaking Gordon's hand. "Pleased to make your acquaintance."

"Likewise," Gordon Longstaff replied.

SKREAAAWK!

Both men startled and immediately looked over at what had made such a terrible and bone-chilling squawking noise in the first place.

What John Scarecrow saw defied description. He'd never seen anything like it before. I was a six-foot-seven-inch lizard creature with the head of a velociraptor and the body of a man, but with scales and leathery skin, a tail, and large bat-like wings. The reptilian monstrosity stood no more than ten feet away from them, fanning its enormous bat-like wings.

"What in the world is that?!"

"Goddammit," the cowboy grumbled, climbing to his feet. Drawing out his .44 Magnum, he added, "If it ain't one thing, it's."

Before he could even get a lock on the giant lizard creature, the beast flapped its wings and swiftly flew across the space between them. Its stone-equipped foot dug into the dirt, kicking up a dust and sand cloud. Suddenly, the creature was standing before the shocked-looking cowboy.

With lightning quick speed, the monster lashed out, swatted the cowboy away, and sent him flying like a ragdoll.

Scarecrow stood up and walked in a circle around the monster, examining it cautiously. "Fascinating."

Coming face-to-face with the creature, Scarecrow asked, "Do you understand my words?"

With its velociraptor head on its humanoid form, the lizard creature leaned in and let out an ear-rattling squawk. Its gnarly breath blew Scarecrow's starchy, yarn-like hair back on his head, and, along with the dinosaur-like screech, came a spray of sputum that speckled Scarecrow's face.

Wiping himself off with a handkerchief he retrieved from his pocket, Scarecrow examined the green ooze and raised an eyebrow. "I guess not."

Just then, the cowboy flew out of nowhere and tackled the creature to the ground. Dust shot up past the two of them, hit the dirt, and somersaulted to a halt. Landing on top, the cowboy made the lizard man into his punching bag and pummeled the beast in the face with everything he had.

Scarecrow cringed at the sound of the knuckle-shattering punches. He was almost sure the cowboy had shattered every bone in his hands in his desperate volley of no-holds-barred punches.

No matter how hard he hit the beast, it didn't matter. The lizard creature just absorbed the punches. Then, in a powerful smack of the beast's leathery elbow, he sent the stuffed-up cowpoke flying to the ground.

The cowboy crashed onto the ground with a thud and then pushed himself up. He rubbed his aching jaw and then looked over at Scarecrow. "You better get yourself clear of here while you can."

Before either of them had time to react, however, the ground.

"*Arrrrgh!*" Gordon groaned. The monster's vice-like grip was painful, like having your skull crushed in. And having his full body weight favors neither.

"I'm sorry, but I can't let you harm him." John Scarecrow drew his own .44 Magnum and aimed it at the lizard man. "Now, I give you fair warning," Scarecrow said, pulling back the hammer on his revolver. "Either you or your head must be off, and that in about half the time! Take your choice!"

Its serpentine yellow eyes fixed on Scarecrow's gun with startling precision. Its black diamond-shaped pupils dilated as they focused on the new threat, and then the creature hissed at Scarecrow as if to warn him to stay back.

The lizard monster tossed the cowboy out of the way, then turned toward Scarecrow and fanned its wings to intimidate him with its alarming size. Throwing out its arms, the lizard monster flexed its razor-sharp claws and growled so loudly that its throat rattled. Scarecrow imagined it sounded rather like what a dinosaur must have sounded like.

"I don't want to hurt you," Scarecrow warned. But trying to reason with the creature was like trying to reason with a brick wall. The moral being, if faced with an oncoming collision with a brick wall, you don't reason with it, you get the heck out of its way or else brace for impact.

Suddenly, the scaly-winged beast lunged at Scarecrow. With its sharp claws, the lizard lashed out but swiped only empty air. Confused, it stopped to look around, but the silly straw man had vanished before its eyes.

"Wow, you move fast," said a voice from behind.

Startled, the creatures spun around and hissed again. It seemed more cautious, as if it was waiting for Scarecrow to make the next move.

Scarecrow stood examining the tears in his suit. "I have to say, that's the first time I've ever been tagged. Quite impressive."

Without warning, the lizard creature flapped its wings and rushed forward, charging with the speed of a bull. But again, its claw only found empty air.

Checking the bullet count in his revolver, Scarecrow spun the chamber and slapped it back into place with a wrist flick. "I tried the carrot. Now let's try the stick."

Raising the gun, Scarecrow steadily aimed it at the creature's head. Getting ready to lunge again, the beast took a step back and prepared for another attack. Its tail fidgeted angrily behind him.

BLAM!

A single shot rang out from the barrel of a gun, and the flash of light was swallowed up in the darkness of the night.

Blood spurted out of the side of the lizard creature's head, and then the beast hit the ground with an unforgiving thud at Scarecrow's feet. This was all very surprising to him since he hadn't pulled the trigger yet.

JohnScarecrowlookedovertoseeGordonLongstaffcradlinghi sribcagewithonearmandholdingasmoking.44Magnumintheoth er. "Sorry to scare you like that, but those things are tougher to kill than an armadillo in Kevlar."

"What was it, anyway?"

The cowboy shrugged, gesturing that he hadn't a clue.

"They're called Nure-Onna," a young girl's voice interjected. "Named after the demonic snake-women as talked about in Japanese folklore."

John Scarecrow and Gordon Longstaff turned to see a Japanese schoolgirl wearing her trademark plaid skirt to go with her school uniform, saunter up with Julie Kingston close at hand.

The Japanese girl glanced at Scarecrow, and said in her thick Japanese accent, "I think I found the one you've been searching for."

24

The Wrong Side of the

Looking Glass

*Somewhere in the Mojave Desert,
northeast of Barstow, California.*

STARING AT JULIE IN DISBELIEF, JOHN SCARECROW
enthusiastically said, "You came back!"

Julie smiled at Scarecrow. "What's the matter? You miss
me?"

"Boy, did I ever!"

"Yeah, I guess I lost my cool back there. It was just so much
to take in. Anyway, Saeko here," Julie said, gesturing to the
young Japanese woman, "is on a mission to find someone's shell
long ago. And, well, she was wondering if I'd be willing to help
her look for her friend."

"And what did you tell her?"

"I said I needed to run it by you first."

The cowboy removed his hat and wiped the sweat off his balding head with a handkerchief. "It's been a long time, Ms. Sakaguchi."

"Not long enough," Saeko snapped, her voice as cold as ice. She glared at Gordon bitterly, then looked away as if she couldn't stand seeing him for a moment longer.

"Look," the cowboy said as he threw out his arms in a gesture of peace. "I didn't want to do what I did, but I had no choice."

"She could have made it. She had made it once before."

"You don't know that," Gordon said, wiping a tear from his eye. "You weren't there. I was."

Saeko just huffed, looked away, folded her arms, and pretended to ignore him.

Julie and Scarecrow, keenly interested in the drama unfolding, turned their backs on their new acquaintances and convened with one.

"So," Julie began, as if the drama that occurred off to the side wasn't happening, "If we're going to be stuck here indefinitely, I thought I'd tag along and lend a helping hand. After all, it's a zombie wonderland, and you know how much I love to shoot things."

"That's true," Scarecrow agreed, rubbing his chin. "You do love to shoot things."

Just then, the sound of footsteps staggering toward them and moaning could be heard—lots of moaning.

Saeko looked back and saw the horde materialize from the dimness. They had multiplied; what began as forty or fifty easily grew to over a hundred. The sound of the gunshot must have alerted them to their presence.

"*Kuso!*" Saeko cursed.

Suddenly, there was the sound of a loud static pop, then the surge of electricity, and the hotel lights came back on.

"Hey!" Scarecrow shouted in excitement. "The hotel is back up and running. That's our ticket out of here."

Julie turned toward Saeko and gave her a sorry look. She didn't feel it was right to abandon their new friends, especially now. Not now. Right now, a horde of flesh-eating monsters had completely surrounded them, and they were, for the lack of a better term, what was for dinner.

Saeko smiled for the first time and said, "Go. Get as far away from this nightmare world as you possibly can. We can't take care of ourselves."

"But I can't leave you, you're just a child..."

Saeko laughed out loud. Then, unable to hold it in, she lost all composure and laughed long, loud, and hard. She hadn't laughed so hard in years. After catching her breath, she said, "Lady, you're sweet, but I'm that you might call an immortal. I may only look sixteen, but I'm twenty-four years old. I haven't aged a day since the outbreak."

"It must be the genes," Scarecrow quibbled.

"Oh," Julie said, somewhat mystified.

Saeko strode up to Julie, her hips swiveling with a seductive sashay, reached around to the back of Julie's neck, grabbed her firmly, pulled her toward her lips, and kissed her.

As the purple of Saeko's lips pressed against the soft pink of Julie's, Scarecrow let out a sigh. The cowboy put his hand on Scarecrow's shoulder to let him know he was right there with him.

After the long, wet kiss, Julie looked into the young woman's deep brown eyes and asked, "What was that for?"

"For reminding me how good it feels to laugh."

Scarecrow looked over at Gordon Longstaff and smiled a chummy grin.

"Don't look at me, padre. I ain't kissing' yah."

Nodding politely, as if to say farewell, Scarecrow turned and took Julie by her arm and tugged at it. "Come along, the clock is sticking, and we haven't any more time to spare. The rabbit hole won't stay open forever."

"Wait," Julie said, breaking free of his grasp. Quickly, Julie unbuckled her gun holster, slipped it off her shoulder, and gave Saeko her Glock G41 with the additional clip. Then she reached behind her back and slid out the Colt Delta Elite that was stuck in the waist area of her pants just above the small of her back. "Take these, you need them more than I do."

Accepting the gifts, Saeko bowed ever so politely. "*Domo arigato gozai-masu.*"

The cowboy looked at Scarecrow, then at his newer, shinier .44 Magnum and grinned .44 Magnum and grinned mischievously, as if he had a yen for it.

"Don't look at me, pal," Scarecrow said, patting his gun like a beloved pet. "This is a classic."

"Fair enough," the cowboy said, chuckling to himself.

Julie nodded toward the old, broken-down cars sitting several meters away, and added, "If you check the glove box, there should be a case of unused bullets. If the plastic wraps survived the weather, you should find them in mint condition."

"Again, thanks for everything," Saeko said, and she bowed more deeply this time.

"GRAAAH!" a monster's voice growled.

A hand reached out of the darkness to pull Julie in, but Saeko leaped into action before it could dig its splintered nails into her. Spinning around, Saeko used her hip to push Julie out of the way, then there was a white-hot flash, the swooshing sound of her blade as it cut through the air, followed by the zombie's dead body hitting the ground. Its face and torso were sliced down the middle.

Just as soon as the zombie had hit the ground, there was another to take its place. This time, it was a curly-haired, blonde woman in a blue waitress's apron, stained with bloody handprints. Her face was peeled halfway off, revealing the frightening outline of teeth and exposed jowls.

Saeko swiped her sword upward and took the woman's head off at the neck. As the head hit the ground, Saeko smashed it with the heel of her boot. Satisfied that they were again in the clear, at least for the time being, Saeko flicked the blood off her sword and sheathed it.

"She's like a ninja!" Scarecrow said admiringly. He was impressed by Saeko's exceptional zombie-slaying skills. And he could tell by the look on Julie's a little bit envious, too.

Saeko turned back toward Julie. "Go," she insisted. "We'll be fine. Trust me, this old-timer and I have survived far worse."

Moans seeped out of the darkness from all sides, and suddenly, four more zombies were bearing down on them. Without hesitating, Scarecrow and the cowboy came together and formed a circle. Standing back-to-back, they drew out their revolvers and began blowing their heads off of the cluster of infected. One by one, the monsters dropped to the ground.

But they weren't out of the woods yet, for just as they'd taken care of the first batch of 20 zombies, suddenly another 20 appeared in their place.

"Let's carve you a path," Gordon said. With a flick of his wrist, he flipped open his revolver, emptied the spent casings, then started to feed fresh shells into the chamber. Once he'd finished reloading, he cocked the hammer back and took aim.

Gordon scanned the area for every threat between the man and the hotel. He slowly squeezed down on the trigger and, with a steely gaze, began blasting zombie skulls left and right.

The .44 Magnum's rounds tore into the walking dead left and right, their heads exploded like water balloons. A mist of red tomato juice lit up in the gunfire as if a zombie bit the dust.

Liking his style, Julie smiled and Drew's sub-compact G36 Glock. It was her third backup gun since she was all about redundancy regarding firearms. Joining the skirmish, she blasted away at the undead.

All around them, muzzle flashes lit up the darkness with a staccato-like consistency. With each blast, there was more blood, until it seemed like a raspberry haze lingered in the air.

In his best Vaudevillian voice, John Scarecrow shouted above the din of gunfire, "See how eagerly the lobsters and the turtles all advance! They are waiting on the shingle—will you join the dance?"

Once all the threats between them and the hotel had been sufficiently gunned down, the shooting finally died down, and Julie let out a sigh of relief.

"More will be becoming," Saeko said, urging them to hurry up and get going.

Suddenly, the hotel lights began flickering, turning off and on sporadically, as if the hotel possessed a fit.

"That's our queue," Scarecrow yelled out.

"Get out of her, now!" Saeko ordered. "There's no more time!"

Julien nodded in affirmation and then turned and ran with Scarecrow back toward the hotel.

As they fled toward the doors, the sound of additional gunshots followed them all the way while the flash gunfire lit up the desert scenery, revealing a horde of the living dead all around them.

Scarecrow pulled open the double-standing door to the hotel entrance and looked back to catch Julie glancing over her shoulder at their new friends. She still felt terrible that they had to leave them to fend for themselves in a world turned on its head.

"You did the right thing," John said.

"Then why doesn't it feel that way?" Julie whispered. It was a miserable feeling having to leave someone behind, not knowing if they'd die or not.

Taking her hand in his, he squeezed it affectionately, and Julie turned back and smiled a morose smile.

"Shall we?" Scarecrow asked. Julie nodded yes, and together they stepped through the hot doors.

FZZZWAT!!

HEAD THROBBING, JULIE RUBBED HER TEMPLES AND OPENED her eyes. It felt as though she'd been run over by a truck. That's when she realized she was lying on her back with Scarecrow's unconscious body lumped over her. Shattered glass from the chandelier lay all around them.

Pushing him off her, she sat up and looked around the room. She saw the remains of the shattered crystal and glass and the old, ramshackle interior of the hotel. She wagered that the chandelier must have knocked her unconscious. Briefly recollecting the events that had transpired, she thought what a strange dream.

Suddenly, Scarecrow sat up in the awkward way he always did when he woke up in the morning, back straight and stiff as a board, like a vampire rising from an open casket. "Wow! That was wild."

"Okay, Steve Martin, just help me up and let's find that mystery girl of yours."

Helping Julie to her feet, Scarecrow smiled pleasantly and asked, "What mystery girl?"

"The girl from the telephone call. The one you were so worried about because you thought she might be the victim of a child abduction."

"Oh, yeah, right. *That girl.*"

"You have no idea who I'm talking about, do you?"

"Not a clue."

Shivering,

Julie wrapped her arms around herself, squishing her breasts together and making her cleavage bulged, rising out of the top of her tank top. Returning to the exit, Julie said, "Remind me why we came out here again."

"Are you kidding me?" Scarecrow said in a flabbergasted, yet over-theatrical voice. "Why, it's our honeymoon, of course!"

Without looking back, Julie muttered an unenthusiastic, "*Ha-ha.*"

"*What?* I'm marriage material!" Scarecrow jested.

"No. What you are is a pain in the ass," Julie retorted. Stepping outside, Julie looked up at the evening sky of the Mojave Desert. "So beautiful," she said to herself.

Following her out into the refreshing night air, Scarecrow added, "Sure is. But maybe not as beautiful as that Asian chick you were tongue wrestling with back there. What will your girlfriend think?"

Spinning around, Julie looked at Scarecrow in dismay. "You mean to tell me... all of that... was real?"

Scratching his chin, he thought about it for a moment. "Well, yes."

"But you don't recall the ghost girl who called you to the haunted hotel in the middle of nowhere?"

Scarecrow scratched his chin as he gazed off into space and thought about it even harder. "*Ummm...*no," he finally revealed, having given it ample thought.

Shrugging, Julie gave up pretending she could understand the workings of the mysterious mind of a supernatural scarecrow. She decided it was best to forget about the whole thing. Besides, it wasn't like anyone would believe her story anyway—not in a million years.

Returning to her beautiful cherry red '65 Mustang, Julie ran her fingertips seductively along the deep red, glossy hood. Starting it up, the soothing rumble of the engines soothed her frayed nerves. Scarecrow parked himself next to her in the passenger seat, smiling his trademark dopey scarecrow grin.

Noticing him staring at her from the corner of her eye, she smiled and returned his gaze. "What's it?"

"I was just wondering what you were thinking."

Snapping her fingers, as if an idea had sprung to mind, she said, "Hey, flip open that glove compartment real quick."

Scarecrow opened the glove box, and they both peered inside. "It's empty," he informed.

Julie smiled.

"Hey, do you think this means what I think it means? Or, more accurately, do you think it means what I think you think I think it means?"

"I'm not entirely sure. But I will tell you this much," Julie said with a wink, "she was one hell of a good kisser."

Scarecrow's eyes grew cartoonishly big, which caused Julie to kick back her head with laughter. Regaining composure, she hit the start button, stepped down on the clutch, shifted the car into first gear, and started back to L.A. — nothing but the gentle rumble of the engine to fill the silent desert night.

FINIS

Acknowledgments

IN THE SUMMER OF 2002, MY FATHER RENTED A STUDIO flat in New York City for an entire month so that we might visit my younger brother, who was attending the prestigious New York Film Academy. My father rented a sublet apartment that, to my great joy, was two blocks from Washington Square Park and the NYCU school library.

During my leisure time, much of which I spent sitting around the park with my sketchbook, I began to fill the pages with images of a scarecrow wearing a fedora and a raincoat. Why scarecrow? Why a fedora? Why a raincoat? I have no idea. That's just what came to me at that particular moment.

When I was thinking up a fantastic story to put that wily scarecrow into, I spent my free time browsing the local bookstores and comic shops, searching for the inspiration that might lead to a kernel of an idea for a story that would suit this strange and fabulous Scarecrow.

This book is the product of that vacation and my time in the Big Apple, and this is the story of that random scarecrow that appeared on that warm afternoon in New York City.

I am grateful to my father for taking me along with him on the journey, even though his journey ended prematurely in May of 2013, just a month before *The Scarecrow an₁ La₁y Kingston* was published.

It is...was... because of my father's never-ending encouragement and support that this book—its story and characters—was even possible, and I'm dedicating it to him. I am deeply saddened that I never got to read it.

Before I close out the acknowledgments, I should briefly explain the bonus story. *The BITTEN x Scarecrow & La₁y Kingston* crossover story was a unique story meant for an anthology series, which was going to be published by Winlock Press, my former publisher. When that gig dried up, I had a nice Scarecrow & Lady Kingston story sitting around for the longest time that I didn't know what to do with.

At about three times the length of a regular short story, it was too short for a novel and too long for anything but an ongoing anthology collection. Even so, once I regained the right to my BITTEN series, I published it as part of this release.

This is the first time this never-before-seen story has appeared in print. I hope you enjoyed reading it.

Finally, I'd like to thank my wife and children, who were more than patient with me as I frantically recompiled, edited, and republished all my books after regaining the rights. Having to do it all over again in double time so as not to miss out on potential sales meant I was practically working full-time on book stuff for a couple of very long months. I thank them for their patience and continued support.

I know my daughter, Solara, will be happy to have "Daddy time" back, as she calls it. Thanks for being patient, kiddo. Daddy loves you and your brother very much! (Note that my youngest son wasn't born yet when this book was written. I love all three of my children equally, but in different ways.)

Also, if you liked this book, please leave a review. Good or bad, your review matters—and can be the difference between whether a series grows more successful or falls into obscurity.

OTHER WORKS BY TRISTAN VICK

NOVELS

The Scarecrow & Lady Kingston
The Chronicles of Jegra 1-6
Valandra 1-3
Bitten 1-3

COMICS

The Astonishing Adventures of Alicia Carter & Robot
The Viking Berserker ZARNA
Daughter of Wolves
Animal Woman
The Profane

www.regolithcomics.com

REGOLITH
PUBLICATIONS

www.ingramcontent.com/pod-product-compliance
Lightning Source LLC
Chambersburg PA
CBHW060549260626
47161CB00003B/1120